ANOTHER MAN'S CITY

CH'OE IN-HO

ANOTHER MAN'S CITY

A NOVEL TRANSLATED FROM THE KOREAN BY BRUCE AND JU-CHAN FULTON

DALKEY ARCHIVE PRESS
Champaign / London / Dublin

First published in Korean as *Nanigŭn t'ain tŭr ŭi toshi*
Copyright ©2011 by Yeoback Media
Translation copyright ©2014 by Bruce & Ju-chan Fulton

First edition, 2014

Library of Congress Cataloging-in-Publication Data

Ch'oe, In-ho, 1945-
  [Nat igun t'aindul ui tosi. English]
  Another man's city / Ch'oe In-ho ; translated from the Korean
by Bruce and Ju-Chan Fulton. -- First edition.
      pages cm
  ISBN 978-1-62897-101-9 (pbk. : alk. paper)
  I. Fulton, Bruce, translator. II. Fulton, Ju-Chan, translator. III. Title.
  PL992.18.I45N3813 2014
  895.73'4--dc23

                          2014016347

Library of Korean Literature

Partially funded by the Illinois Arts Council, a state agency
Published in collaboration with the Literature Translation
Institute of Korea

www.dalkeyarchive.com

Cover: design and composition by Mikhail Iliatov
Printed on permanent/durable acid-free paper

Ch'oe In-ho (1945-2013) will go down in Korean literary history as the writer who breathed new life into modern fiction on the peninsula—a tradition that was in danger of being stunted by the powerful South Korean literary establishment and its preference for a literature that bears explicit witness to the sobering realities of life before South Korea became the high-tech giant it is today. He was only seventeen when he made his formal literary debut, earning one of the annual new writer prizes sponsored by the Seoul daily newspapers. The story is well known of the boy in his black, high-school uniform appearing at the award ceremony and being asked by the master of ceremonies, "Where's your big brother?"

In fact, his big brother was the source of his school uniforms and other clothing during their middle and high school years. Their father died when In-ho was ten (an experience described in his story "Dead Person" [1974, translated in *Acta Koreana* December 2008]), leaving his widow and six children in poverty. Young In-ho was nicknamed "Raggedy" for the state of his clothing. Writing, he determined early on, would be his escape from such straitened circumstances. He read widely, his favorite authors ranging from Kim Yu-jŏng, a delightful voice from colonial Korea, to Rilke, and to Truman Capote.

After completing his obligatory military service (in the ROK Air Force) and earning a degree in English literature from Yonsei University in Seoul, Ch'oe quickly became a full-time writer. Before the age of 30 he had published two of his signature surrealist stories, "The Boozer" (1970, translated in *Land of Exile*, revised and expanded edition, 2007) and "Another Man's Room" (1971, translated in *Modern Korean Fiction*, 2005). Two novels published in 1973, *Homeland of the Stars* and *Procession of Fools*, cemented his reputation among a younger generation of readers. So popular was he by then that the Korean press funded him on an around-the-world sightseeing trip, from which he dispatched daily reports back to Seoul. He was the first Korean fiction writer whose face adorned, not the book jacket, but the cover of his books. More of his works (nineteen) were made into films (he also wrote screenplays) than the works of any other ROK writer, and those early followers remained loyal to him for his entire fifty-year career.

What accounted for this popularity? Despite his credentials—born in the capital of Seoul, coming of age during the April 1960 student revolution that forced the resignation of heavy-handed President Syngman Rhee, majoring in a foreign literature at one of the nation's most prestigious universities, employing in his writing a vocabulary heavy with Sino-Korean words (think of an English-language writer relying heavily on words with Latin rather than Anglo-Saxon origins)—Ch'oe was a writer of the people. He was a visual writer with imagination and humor, qualities readers thirsted for in the parched and repressive climate of South Korean military dictatorships from 1961 through 1987. He located the bizarre, the laughable, and the comic in daily life, readers seeing in themselves the foibles Ch'oe picked at with gentle humor in his fiction. His stories routinely appeared in quality literary journals, and his novels were serialized in the newspapers, with the exception of *Family*, which appeared in monthly installments in the magazine *Saemt'ŏ* for more than 34 years—a record in South Korean publishing. He was a daily presence in the South Korean popular imagination, second in readers' affections only to the late Pak Wan-sŏ among writers of literary fiction.

In the early 1980s a crisis of confidence and the repressive military dictatorship prompted him to depart for a road trip in Southern California, the background of his 1982 Yi Sang Prize-winning story "Deep Blue Night" (translated in *Deep Blue Night*, 2002). Already, by then, he had developed a lifelong association with the Saemt'ŏ publishing company, at whose offices he did much of his creative writing.

Although a devout Catholic, he had a profound interest in Buddhism, reflected in his three-volume novel *Way Without a Way* (1991). His syncretic world-view informed his fiction until his death, another factor in his great popularity.

Another Man's City (literally, "The City of Familiar Others," 2011) was composed after an initial bout of the throat cancer that ultimately claimed his life, and was honored with the Kim Tongni Literature Prize. It was a novel he had long been fashioning in his mind, and he finished the first draft in two months, writing as usual by hand, but with thumb and fingertip thimble guards, his fingernails and hair having been lost to chemotherapy and radiation treatments. In one of his last public statements he declared that he wished to be recalled as a writer and not a cancer victim, and that *Another Man's City* was the novel he wanted to be remembered by.

Our relationship with Ch'oe goes back to the mid-1990s, when we translated his wonderful, magical-realist sketch "The Poplar Tree" for *Morning Calm*, the in-flight magazine of Korean Air, and then "Deep Blue Night." We hosted him on two International Communication Foundation-sponsored reading tours of North America, during which he was paired first with the afore-mentioned Pak Wan-sŏ, and the following year with the current elder stateswoman of Korean fiction, O Chŏng-hŭi. He was a hit with students at home and abroad, especially at the University of British Columbia, where a 1999 appearance with Pak Wan-sŏ drew a standing-room-only audience of a hundred-plus in a space designed for half that number. Several of his stories have been translated by UBC students, who continue to find his style engaging and accessible.

Ch'oe In-ho was a devoted family man, a deeply spiritual man who also enjoyed fine cigars and drink, and a compassionate and loving friend. He fought cancer with dignity and courage. And like another giant of modern Korean literature, Hwang Sun-wŏn, he trusted in us absolutely. It is with great affection that we dedicate this translation to his memory.

— *Bruce and Ju-Chan Fulton*

ANOTHER MAN'S CITY

SATURDAY

7 a.m.

(POWER ON)

What the hell? K groped the fuzzy boundary between sleep and wakefulness for an answer—what had awakened him?

His alarm clock. The strident ring a desperate cry letting the world know of its existence. Again the shrill clamor.

Dammit! K didn't like being woken up. He fumbled at the nightstand, found the alarm clock, silenced it.

He wasn't fully awake. But he was conscious enough to splice the snapped filmstrip of his interrupted sleep, and he closed his eyes.

Hey! The alarm was telling him it was time to get up. He forced his eyes open, checked the display on the clock. 7 a.m. sharp. 7 a.m. He groaned. Time to rise. Time to get his butt in gear—get up, get ready, get off to work. He sat up.

Wait. Something wasn't right. Wasn't it Saturday? Saturday—he didn't have to go to work. Saturday—a day of privilege, a day he slept in, had a leisurely breakfast, lazed around.

Sure, it's Saturday, right? he clucked, easing himself back into bed. He grabbed at the elusive remnant of his sleep, felt it twitch like the severed tail of a lizard.

It's Saturday all right. Which meant he'd been out late last night drinking with H, right? And come home and made love with his wife, right? No day off the following day, no sex with his wife the night before. For K it was a rule inscribed in stone.

"The Friday night festival, you and me," he would whisper. Their cue for lovemaking. The next day had to be a day off. Otherwise it was too much work, it took too much out of him. That they'd done it last night was clear proof that today was a day off.

And so... The lizard tail of his dream was no longer twitching. It had disappeared into the magic forest of dreamland. So much for the possibility of going back to sleep.

But if today was Saturday, he should be able to sleep in. So why the alarm? Way back then, he used to set the alarm for seven so he wouldn't be late for work. But these days he rarely bothered.

If he didn't get up right on time, his wife was there to awaken him, right? So who had set the alarm to go off on a Saturday morning? His wife? Couldn't be. She was helpless with mechanical contrivances, wouldn't dare touch an alarm clock. Which left him.

He closed his eyes, searched his memory. It was a fact that he'd drunk more than usual last night and come home late, but he wasn't so drunk, so witless, that he'd set the alarm for a morning when he didn't have to get up. But if it wasn't him, and it wasn't his wife, then who the hell had managed to interrupt his sleep? Was someone playing mind games?

No sense trying to get back to sleep. So he opened his eyes, sat up, stretched. The curtains were open, sunlight fanning in through the window. From the kitchen came the clatter of dishes and the smell of buttered toast—his wife was up and about, fixing breakfast.

The familiar aroma, the familiar polka-dot pattern of the curtains.

"My room all right," he murmured.

He felt the urge and sprang out of bed, heading for the bathroom. Tapping his full bladder, he watched the yellow stream foam up in the toilet bowl, noticed the alcohol odor. He flushed the toilet, looked up, was startled. There in the mirror, a man without a stitch of clothing. None other than himself, but it took him an extra moment to realize this. The image in the mirror didn't feel like him. He gaped at that image. *That's me?* He was buck naked. And not once in his married life had he ever slept without pajamas.

"Who are you?" he mumbled, glaring at the man in the mirror. "Who's hiding there?" There was no answer, only his voice hanging heavy in the air. And then, realizing how silly the question was, he burst into laughter. "Knock knock, who's there? That's a good one—it's *me*."

The naked, laughing man in the mirror looked obscene. The genitalia beneath the flabby belly resembling the pendulum of a wall clock, his laughter working his body like a metronome.

He chuckled. *Who took my jammies off?* His wife? He shook his head. No, even when they made love, she couldn't abide him being naked. She'd been like that since the day they were married.

"A naked body is revolting, there's something dirty about it.

Makes me think I'm in a butcher shop, looking at a side of beef," she'd say.

And so it was only in pitch darkness that she would agree to foreplay and intercourse. Nor did K want his naked form displayed to anyone, even his wife. Revealing himself was too shameful and embarrassing.

So who left me in my birthday suit? Looking at himself in the mirror, he felt like a plucked chicken.

Maybe he'd shed his pajamas in his sleep? Impossible. Even half-awake, people didn't do that sort of thing, unless they were sleepwalkers or prostitutes.

Where were his pajamas anyway? He returned to the bedroom and looked around. Odds were a million to one his wife hadn't stripped them off of him, but if she had, they'd be somewhere near the bed, folded neatly. He scoured the vicinity. Nothing. No pajamas.

"Honey!"

No response—she was too busy in the kitchen, K figured. Just as well—she'd never seen him naked, and if she did now, she might scream her head off, like he was a pervert exposing himself. He found an undershirt and a pair of briefs in the closet, and threw on an old dress shirt over them.

Back to the bathroom, where he squeezed a large dollop of toothpaste onto his toothbrush and started brushing. He gagged— *all that booze!*—and took aim at the toilet bowl. Out flowed a short stream of sour fluid, toothpaste foam, and saliva. He flushed the toilet and lowered the lid. Back to brushing. K observed his face in the mirror. A familiar face, gloomy splotches of color. A depressing countenance. It didn't sit well with him.

Well, then, how about a shave—just the thing to brighten his appearance. No good getting down in the dumps, especially on a Saturday, especially after a stressful week at work.

With his shaving brush he worked up a generous helping of lather. His face took on the fuzzy look of their puppy. If he didn't shave in the morning, by the end of the day his face would take on a dark shadow, that's how fast his beard grew. His razor began to slice through the lather. An electric shaver would have been faster and easier, but K stuck with his razor, preferring the sharp edge. Cutting mercilessly through his beard offered the same thrill as when just before ejaculation he stopped thrusting and held back the semen that was about to fountain out.

Before he knew it he was whistling. The sound was amplified in the confines of the bathroom, and for an instant he imagined himself soloing the part of "Shadow of a Faded Love" that the singer whistles. But K wasn't one to whistle tunes; improvising was better, giving expression to his mood of the moment.

Oops—he had drawn blood. A frequent occurrence. He stuck a piece of tissue to his chin. There—a nice clean shave. He looked much more cheerful now. With warm water he removed the remnants of lather. Then came a palmful of aftershave. Getting out of bed, washing his face, shaving, combing his hair—among this sequence of tasks, applying aftershave was best. It was the climax of his morning grooming.

The aftershave was strong stuff. It felt like a branding iron on the nicks and scrapes. Then came an electric buzz that left his face momentarily numb. And the fragrance, so powerful he didn't need cologne. He'd used the same aftershave since his bachelor days. It was simply called V. Its scent defined him. *V is me—accept no substitutes.*

But something was amiss. He held up the bottle, examined the label. Y. Not V but Y. A brand he'd never used, had never seen before.

How could it be? As far back as he could remember, V was his one and only aftershave, the one he had used yesterday, the day before, a week and a half ago, last month, last year, years back, even before he was married. V was his brand, his trademark. It had to be somewhere. He examined his toiletries. They were kept in a ceramic bowl on the counter next to the sink. A gift he and his fellow church members had received on the tenth anniversary of the church; it was inscribed "God Is Love." To one side of the bowl were his toothbrush and toothpaste, a selection of Q-tips, his nail clippers, his electric nose-hair clippers, Mercurochrome and other first-aid items, the moisturizer he occasionally applied after his shower, as well as air freshener for the bathroom. They were all where they were supposed to be, just as he'd arranged them. This was his very own space, the sink and mirror and drawer. His wife kept her toiletries in her vanity case.

He checked the washstand drawer. Everything in place there as well, everything where he had put it. K liked to organize things, and was peeved if they weren't where they ought to be. In the back of the drawer were the condoms and other contraceptives, as well as the sample of erectile dysfunction medication he'd been given by his doctor friend H. K had tucked it away for emergency use, unbeknownst to his wife.

He glanced at the pills, two of them, blue, secured in clear cellophane. *Damn*, he clucked. *If only I'd remembered them last night.*

After coming home drunk, he'd signaled his wife that it was festival time. And she had obliged. Unless something unavoidable came up, Friday nights were reserved for the two of them—that was the agreement.

Even though they made love in deep-sea darkness, it was not that his wife didn't take pleasure from it. He could feel, as his wife built toward climax, the temperature of her seething body skyrocket when he entered her. And when she came, he could almost see her light up like a phosphorescent fish.

But last night had been a dud—he couldn't get an erection, hadn't been able to complete the act. Never in their marriage had this happened. Her body had felt ice cold. How to describe it? It was like caressing a dead body, a cold-blooded creature. He remembered passing his hand across the cheek of his mother just before she was encoffined—his wife had felt even colder. The frigidity of marble, of ice, of an inanimate object—that's how his wife's body had felt. He had thought for a moment he was in bed with a corpse. This was supposed to be their love life, their bed—it wasn't a butcher shop, he wasn't raping her, he wasn't some pervert, some necrophiliac.

"Honey, what is it?" she had asked, her voice importunate in the dark room, where no light penetrated the curtains.

"Can't get it up."

"You must be tired. And you probably drank too much, didn't you?"

Looking now at the pair of blue pills, K was seized with regret. If only he'd remembered, he could have taken them on the sly, then given it another try.

But it wasn't those pills he was looking for, it was his after-shave. Where was it? He considered the possibilities. Someone had taken it—and replaced it. His wife? Couldn't be. He was the one who purchased his aftershave, she had nothing to do with it. Which would leave K as the culprit. *Am I playing a trick on myself, the old shell game?*

K lifted the toilet lid and sat. Not for the usual reason, but because he needed to make sense of what was going on. Something was messed up. It had started at seven, when the alarm came on. It had come on by itself—nobody had set it. And then, for the first time in his fifteen years of married life, he had risen from his bed naked, his bedclothes having vanished like a magician's dove. And finally his aftershave had disappeared, replaced with a brand he wouldn't be caught dead with.

Where had this string of events begun? Or was he imagining this? No—it was real, and the tricks had started last night. Maybe with the menacing chill he'd felt in reaction to his wife's corpse-like frigidity, killing his accustomed sexual desire. Did that mean his wife, like his aftershave, had been replaced?

He shook his head. Yes, he was under an illusion—the visible world was real but his brain had processed it into something distorted.

K shot to his feet, turned on the shower. Put a hand underneath and the next moment felt the familiar hot water pouring down. *Same hot water as yesterday, thank God.* He turned it off. Now he knew he wasn't hallucinating.

He took a quick shower. As he dried his face with the familiar towel, he saw in the mirror his familiar face, like a reproduction of a portrait. Further proof that he wasn't delusional.

Combing his hair came next, and here he was especially attentive. Streaks of gray had begun appearing, exactly when he couldn't remember. At first he had plucked the offending hairs, but before long it became a losing battle. If he kept removing the gray hair he'd end up practically bald. So why bother? By now he was used to the gray. And today he was no grayer than he'd been yesterday.

There in the mirror, his nose, his lips, his ears—K himself. He examined that face with his small magnifying mirror. Exaggerated, grotesque as a death mask, it was nevertheless his face. But just to make sure, he opened his mouth wide and checked his teeth. There, toward the back, his gold crown. The sight of that familiar molar released him, finally, from his unease. There was no hallucination, no illusion; he wasn't on a stage set or in a make-believe world.

Light of heart and whistling, K went out to the living room. Once he saw the familiar scene of his wife at work in the kitchen, he could bring down the curtain on this shadow play.

8:15 a.m.

His wife was at the sink chopping spinach. For breakfast K typically had salad—lettuce, celery, tomatoes, spinach, broccoli, onions—with a banana thrown in for good measure.

"Good morning, honey."

She didn't hear him over the *tock tock tock*. Instead of repeating himself K poured a mug of coffee and sat down at the table to read his newspaper. He took a sip and savored it. *Good old coffee.*

Between sips he picked up the newspaper. *Explosion at Korean Pipeline in Yemen—Al Qaida Responsible.* The front-page story—the bombing of a Yemeni pipeline operated by Korea Petroleum—complete with a photo of billowing black smoke.

Yemen, Yemen. Was that something he should care about, the roiling flames and billowing smoke in a small country on the Arabian Peninsula, far, far away? He put down the newspaper.

He looked at his wife. Something wasn't quite right. And then it struck him. What was she doing, wearing *his* pajamas? Jade blue with polka dots, the bottoms with their cuffs—definitely his pajamas. The very pajamas whose disappearance had flummoxed him since he'd caught sight of his naked self in the mirror. What in God's name was she doing in his pajamas—had she stripped him?

Honey. Before he could voice the word he was hit with a thought: *Are you sure that woman is your wife?* It was one thing to be stripped of his pajamas, but how dare she wear them herself, and with an insolence he had never seen before. Who the hell was this brazen, shameless woman masquerading as his wife?

He mustered his courage. "Honey?"

She turned to him: "Oh, you're up."

It was his wife, her voice and her face.

"When did you get up?"

"Just now." K faked nonchalance but remained vigilant. "Did you sleep well, honey?"

But she had resumed her chopping and she turned back to K only to say "Yes, I did." Her brief, noncommittal glance gave him the impression that she was playing hide-and-seek with her feelings and he was "it."

K made a show of picking up the newspaper and casually said, "You did something with the alarm clock, right?"

"Excuse me?" she said, not turning back this time.

"Didn't you set it for seven?"

"What are you talking about—I don't even know how to work it."

"Well, somebody worked it, because it woke me up."

"Are you sure *you* didn't do it?"

"Why would I—today's Saturday."

"Well, if you didn't do it, then it must have come on by mistake."

Her matter-of-fact tone came across as dismissive to K. He felt indignant.

"And who took my aftershave?"

"What?" She had just bitten into a chunk of the carrot she'd been laboring over.

"I said, where did my aftershave go?"

"Now dear, who would take your aftershave?"

"*Someone* switched it with *Y.*"

"Y? I've never heard of an aftershave called Y."

"Okay—then how about those pajamas you're wearing—whose are they?"

"Pardon?"

"Those pajamas you're wearing—those are *my* pajamas."

She approached with the salad.

"Oh, these. I threw mine in the wash, and then I saw yours and so I borrowed yours."

"You mean," K mumbled, feeling like an idiot, "you *stripped* me?"

"Who, me?" His wife giggled.

It was strange. A chill was emanating from her, and he felt a sense of alienation. He glared at her but said nothing.

"Why would I strip you? Maybe if I were out of my mind. Maybe I was trying to rape you, is that what you're thinking?"

She said it jokingly but K wasn't in the mood.

Next to the glass bowl of salad she placed buttered toast together with strawberry jam and milk.

"Then who stripped me?"

"Well, you did."

"Me? I took off my pajamas?"

"*Who else?*" And then, "By the way, do you happen to remember what day it is?"

"What day it is? It's Saturday, my day off."

"*Aigo*, my forgetful husband. It's the wedding."

"Wedding?"

"Yes, your dear sister-in-law's wedding. My...sister," she said, stressing both words.

"I totally forgot," K said sheepishly. "What time is it?"

"Twelve noon. We need to hurry. I have to go to the beauty parlor and get made-up."

"*You* need to get made-up? You're not the one getting married."

"Everyone in the bridal party gets made up—you know. So we have to leave by ten. I had your suit dry-cleaned—it's in the closet."

K spread jam over a slice of toast and ate, then had a sip of milk. Then on to the tomatoes and celery. He liked the astringent taste of celery.

"You know..." K tried to read his wife's face before continuing. "I can't figure it out—who took off my pajamas?"

"Well, if it wasn't you, dear, it must have been a ghost."

"Which means you saw me naked."

She gave him a playful slap on the back of his hand and smiled. "Oh, yes, we're just dying to see you and your flab."

K felt a chill—from that slapping hand there came a harrowing hostility. That hand didn't belong to the sweet, familiar wife he knew. It felt cold like the skin of a hibernating reptile, sharp like a scalpel, harsh like a whip.

K struggled to make sense of it. First the alarm clock... then his aftershave... and now *her* in *his* pajamas.

"We need to get going, there's not much time." Taking one last mouthful of breakfast, she went to their daughter's room and called out, "Come on, sweetie, time to get up. We need to get you fixed up."

"I know, Mom," their daughter shouted back. K heard the puppy whimpering in her room. "Just let me sleep a little longer."

"It's your aunt's wedding today."

"I *know*, Mom."

Her voice was petulant and the dog's whimpering was louder.

K had lost his appetite. He got up and, taking what was left of his coffee, went out onto the enclosed balcony. Once he had slid the pair of glass doors shut he was in a space of his own, the noise from inside and out blocked off. A space containing the orchids and other potted plants given to them on the occasion of this anniversary or that and which no one took care of. A space where he could exile himself and indulge in his daily nicotine fix in peace. He allowed himself three cigarettes a day, one in the morning, one at lunchtime, one in the evening. And on special occasions maybe one before bed. But he didn't consider himself addicted—a pack of cigarettes would last him several days easy, sometimes even a week. But this morning, he would allow himself two in a row. He had to get to the bottom of this inexplicable series of events that was causing him such anxiety.

"Just can't understand it," he mumbled as he puffed away.

His wife had passed it all off as a joke, the work of ghosts, but she wasn't telling him the truth. Was she trying to deceive him? Had she set the alarm clock, stripped off his pajamas, and replaced his aftershave? There was no indication that anyone had broken into their apartment. So it had to be his wife. But what did she have to gain by playing tricks on her husband? And what was the purpose of the alibi about the pajamas—she'd sounded so nonchalant, as if it was standard procedure to wear her husband's pajamas while hers were in the wash.

He had half-opened the window to the outside to let out the smoke, and through the opening he heard the honking of cars, and from the middle-school playfield across the street, shouted voices and the uplifting sounds of running feet and kicked soccer balls— the Saturday soccer match featuring the neighborhood team decked out in their uniforms. K saw, on the track encircling the artificial turf, their neighbors from the apartment building wobbling around like wind-up toys. The familiar scene of a familiar Saturday morning. K finished his first cigarette and lit the second.

Once again he wondered about his anxiety. He reminded himself that it was actually last night when the signs started to appear. The ice-cold feel of his wife's frozen body, his inability to achieve an erection. Something had happened last night, but *what?* Puffing on his cigarette, he went over the events of last night one by one. He had left work at 6:30. Set out on foot for the clinic. He had plenty of time—H didn't finish with his patients till seven—so no need to drive. Fifteen minutes by foot would get him there without hurrying. So he took his time, detouring for two blocks along the river. A young couple politely asked if K would photograph them with the man's cell phone. K had ample time but waved them off, saying he was in a hurry. And then, to prove his point, he briskly strode off.

Dusk had settled and the buildings began to glitter. People brushed past one another, coming and going. Someone at a crosswalk was handing out flyers. K wasn't interested until he saw that the flyer came with a sample, a silver breath mint that resembled a ball bearing, and he took it. He popped the mint into his mouth, then crumpled the flyer and dropped it in a bin. The mint was bitter, spicy, and sour, all at the same time—K wished he had something to wash it down with.

A new shop was opening nearby with the help of a bevy of models clad in micro miniskirts who gave a spiel and entertained spectators with their dancing, their skirts so short K half-expected a glimpse of their panties. K noticed the older men among the crowd ogling the curvaceous legs while doing their best to be discreet about it. The models seemed to enjoy the attention. K didn't want to give them the satisfaction, and made a conscious effort to avoid eye contact. He checked his watch—7 p.m. sharp.

Nearing the clinic, he called H to announce his arrival. But the nurse, even though she recognized K's voice and knew he was a friend of H, made a point of asking who was calling. K loathed her attitude, which made him reluctant to visit H at his clinic.

K sensed from the nurse's wife-like behavior that the two of them were having an affair. But he had long since decided to play dumb. This did not sit well with the nurse. K guessed she magnified her resentment in an attempt to impress upon him the nature of her relationship with H—she was more than just a lover, she was almost a wife to him. Knowing the nurse would take on airs if he gave her the satisfaction of acknowledging as much, K feigned indifference all the more. But then came an incident at the clinic, which K now realized was a result of her irritation with him. One day K had dropped by unannounced and found only the nurse at the clinic. She had greeted him with a suggestive glance and asked him in an apologetic but discreet tone to help zip up her uniform. K was perfectly capable of the task, but begged off, saying he had hurt his hand and couldn't move his fingers very well. As luck would have it, he actually had nicked a fingertip that day while sharpening a pencil, and was wearing a Band-Aid. The nurse had given K a sharp look and stormed out. Ever since then she had responded to K's phone calls as she did now:

"I'm sorry but the doctor is out—whom shall I say is calling?"

"This is his friend K," K replied impassively. And then he patiently remained on the line.

Finally H came on. "Why don't you come in?"

K said he would wait outside instead.

"All right, I'll be out as soon as I change."

K noticed a crowd in front of the shop next to the clinic and approached the display window. A few people were photographing the interior with their cell phones. The window held a mannequin. K moved closer to examine it, wondering what had drawn all these people in—after all, all sorts of shops had mannequins. This one was a life-size female, rendered in exquisite detail.

"Hey, I saw its eyelids move!" exclaimed a middle-school kid.

Sure enough, the mannequin was blinking. K realized it wasn't a mannequin, it was a person. An attention-grabbing tactic on the part of the shop, a kind of pantomime. The body remained motionless, but apparently the model couldn't help blinking.

K was getting peeved. Not because he had been slow to pick up on the illusion; rather he found the shallow display of commercialism unpleasant—dressing up a person as a mannequin? And then with wooden movements the mannequin—no, the young woman—turned, opened the door through to the display window, and disappeared into the shop. It must have been a shift change. The onlookers dispersed.

But K patiently observed the window, waiting for the curtain to go up on act two. Presently the door to the window opened and another mannequin appeared, this one a man. He was well built and naked except for his briefs. Posing like a Greek statue of a discus thrower, he showed off his muscles. A college student at a part-time job? No, K decided, he looked more like an exhibitionist parading his handsome physique. The way his genitalia bulged made K wonder if he'd padded his briefs; his oiled body gleamed in the streetlights like a bronze statue. At first the young man drew only stray glances from the people passing by, but soon a flock of women had thronged to the window to photograph him with their cell phones. K couldn't understand their excited chatter but assumed they were Chinese or Japanese.

And then he felt a tap on his shoulder.

"Sorry to keep you waiting," said H.

K turned to find H and the nurse, who was studiously avoiding him.

"How about some dinner? A pot of stew and some nice warm *chŏngjong* to burn off the chill?"

K was not pleased that H had brought the nurse. She had linked arms with H in a pose that was obviously for public consumption. *What a ridiculous-looking pair*, thought K, the rotund H linking arms with the lanky nurse. *They belong in a movie.*

They found a *shabu-shabu* restaurant nearby and placed their order. The *chŏngjong* arrived—a blowfish fin was steeping in the ceramic pot—and they all had a drink. In the presence of the nurse, K kept his silence. The *chŏngjong* was too warm and he broke out in a sweat.

The meal had lasted an hour or so, and K didn't remember much about it except for when H left for the men's room and the nurse surprised him with a question.

"Do you love your wife?"

K thought he understood the motive behind the abrupt question. The nurse, well aware of K's annoyance with her, must have felt it necessary to remind K that her affair with H was a kind of charity work, an attempt to comfort an unhappily married man. K knew that a no from him would serve to justify the nurse's part in the affair, whereas a yes would acknowledge H's shadiness.

"Well, I'm not quite sure how to answer that."

The nurse dug deeper. "Do you think you are a moralist, Mr. K?"

Moralist? You mean am I ethical? Silently K snorted—once again he'd been caught off guard. He gulped his still-hot *chŏngjong*. He was most definitely not a moralist. But even if he were, his disdain for the nurse was not a matter of judging his friend's secret liaison as an ethical right or wrong. Rather it was the nurse's coquettishness unbefitting her age, her look-what-I've-got attitude with regard to H, and her playing the faithful wife to him—it was so patently an act.

"I'm not a *moralist*," said K, deliberately using the English word.

The conversation, such as it was, ended when H returned. H, knowing K didn't like the nurse's presence, dispatched her in a taxi as soon as they had finished their meal. But not before they shared a quick kiss as K looked the other way.

"Love you," whispered the nurse in H's ear, loud enough for K to hear. Two drinks of *chŏngjong* and already she was slurring her words.

As soon as the taxi disappeared, H spat.

"Crazy bitch." He clenched his teeth. "Filthy whore... Let's you and me have a drink. I found this great new place."

K wasn't really in the mood, but he had nothing better in mind, so he nodded. It was still early, only a little past 8 p.m. Why go home now? Besides, tomorrow was a day off.

K had paid for dinner, so H would take care of the drinks. They caught a taxi, and H gave directions to the driver.

They had known each other since high school, but had little opportunity to develop their relationship during college and had not been close. It was only recently that they had renewed contact, K seeking out H because of his wife's fixations. Since early in their marriage her anxiety had manifested itself in blinking as well as a face-twitching tic. And every time she left the apartment she first went through an endless routine of checking that she'd turned off the gas to the stove, unplugged the iron, locked the door — it was a compulsion she couldn't get rid of. When her symptoms intensified, K looked though the alumni directory for a psychiatrist and found H. But after two months of treatment she decided to discontinue the visits.

Surprisingly H had supported her decision. "I guess she needs to be patient and deal with it on her own. Medication won't necessarily help," he had said to K, who had sought him out to express his regrets about his wife's decision. K found H's attitude to his liking. And then before he knew it, their roles were reversed. K happened to be sitting in the doctor's seat while H, sprawled across the sofa, began to lament his own situation. His wife was playing around. At first she'd done it behind his back, but now everything was out in the open — the occasional night out with the man, his phone calls, his face adorning the screen of her cell phone. Sure, her behavior drove him up the wall, but what really hurt was her lack of respect—it was humiliating.

"Crazy bitch," he spat. "Filthy whore."

K merely listened — how should he respond to someone he wasn't that close to, venting like this?

"Dirty fucking whore. Goddamned bitch."

What was that moisture on H's cheeks — tears? No, more like a thin film of cleansing lotion. Maybe it was perspiration?

"Some day I'll kill the bitch, and that SOB too," he said, glaring at K.

K could tell that H wouldn't hurt a fly, much less resort to violence. Instead he would probably get dumped by his wife. And that's the day they became friends—but not so much through affinity as through a shared secret.

"One of these days you can meet her," said H.

But K never had. Which sometimes made him suspect H was actually single and his suffering paradoxically all in his head, the result of having tended to so many patients with their various problems. Maybe his wife's infidelity was part of a confession he'd manufactured to rationalize his illicit affair with the nurse, similar to the fantasy experienced by some women who want to have a baby and who convince themselves they're pregnant. In any event, it was H's wife's nymphomania, squalid and shameless, that proved to be the pivot of the two men's friendship.

K had no clue where the taxi was taking them, didn't recognize the place they were let out. H seemed to know where he was going and set off along a dark street before turning down an alley. K was tipsy from gulping the overly warm *chŏngjong*.

The place they came to was like a darkroom, faces impossible to distinguish. K wondered why it was so dark—was something wrong with the lighting? H asked a hostess for his whiskey—he must be keeping a bottle there. The two men didn't talk much, mostly drank while watching a couple locked together on the small dance floor. Their sensual pose made them look like performers in a strip show.

K didn't remember much of what H said, only that he kept cursing his wife. She had asked him for a divorce, and he had flatly refused. Not that he had a lingering attachment to her—there was just no way he would give her the satisfaction of being free and clear. He would wait until the SOB dumped her, then he himself would pop the divorce question when she came crawling back. He had enough dirt on her to throw her out without a dime, that's what she'd get for her disgraceful affair. H punctuated each of these declarations by downing a shot of whiskey and hurling a "Crazy bitch!" or "Dirty whore!"

And then the woman on the dance floor invited H to dance. He staggered out to the floor and began a slow dance with her. K glimpsed him feeling up the woman's thigh through the hip-high slit in her *qipao*. Next the woman came for K, whether for a drink or a dance he couldn't recall, and then things got more blurry, except he vaguely remembered the woman slathering him with attention.

And what happened after that? K now asked himself as he finished his cigarette on the balcony. But the filmstrip of his memory had snapped at that point, and it wasn't until eleven or so, when he was getting out of a taxi at his apartment, that it was spliced back together. The best he could remember, he and H had left the restaurant shortly after eight, arrived at the bar around 8:30, and were there until 9:30.

Which left a vacuum in his memory between 9:30 and 11:00. What could have happened during that hour and a half? Was he dancing with that spider woman, who clung to him like a web? Had H stayed beside him the whole time, looking out for him, then loaded him in a taxi and sent him home? Otherwise, in his pickled, drink-addled state, he would have ended up passed out on the street. *What* had happened to him during that blank period? The sensation of his wife's frigid, corpse-like body during the festival—was that part of the enigma? And the confusing mishaps this morning—were they also connected with last night's mystery?

He had to call H. Where was his cell phone—that's where H's number was stored. Into the bedroom he went. He fumbled in the pockets of his clothes. Where the hell was it? Not in his jacket, not in his pants. Now what? All the important information was in that cell phone—the phone numbers of business associates, the personal information about the important people in his life. It would be a disaster if he'd lost his phone. He searched his pockets once more, then rushed out to the kitchen. His wife had finished the dishes and was sitting over a cup of coffee at the table.

"Have you seen my cell phone, honey?"

"What?"

"My cell phone—have you seen it?"

"No, I haven't—you can't find it?"

"No."

"Did you look everywhere?" she asked. It didn't seem that important to her. "It has to be somewhere—unless you lost it."

"It's not here—I checked all my pockets."

Her expression lit up. "Why don't you call yourself. If your phone's here we'll hear the ring, if not, then you left it somewhere—or you lost it."

She was right. K picked up the receiver. Another problem—he'd never called himself on his cell phone, and couldn't remember the number. He had to ask his wife, and then he stabbed at the number pad. Through the receiver he heard the familiar ring. But could he hear it here in the apartment? He strained to listen. His phone had to be ringing somewhere—but it wasn't ringing here.

"I don't hear it," she said. "Do you?"

"No."

"That's odd," she muttered. "We talked on it last night, didn't we?"

This was news to K. He had no memory of talking with her then.

"Let's see, I think it was around ten. I asked when you were coming home."

If it was around ten, the call must have fallen into that hour-and-a-half dead zone.

"So what did I say?"

"That you'd be home soon—don't you remember? Where were you, anyway? It must have been a bar—I could hear music and noise in the background."

"Yeah, I think it was a bar."

"Then you must have left it there. Who were you with?"

"I was with H."

"Then either you left it there or he has it. Why don't you give him a call."

"I don't know his number—it's on my phone."

"Well, you'll get it back. The call you just made will show up on your phone, and whoever has it—unless he stole it—can contact you and give it back. So let's be patient."

Their daughter, MS, appeared, yawning. She must have just gotten up. She came up to K for her morning hug. "Good morning,

Daddy," she said in her singsong tone.

K cringed at his daughter's display of affection. It was a creepy feeling, as if he'd touched an insect. But why?

"Get a move on," his wife said to her. "We need to leave by ten." And then to K, "You too, honey. You need to take us to the hair salon."

Just then MS's puppy appeared. Seeing K, it growled and bared its teeth. Because K was allergic to animal fur, the puppy was kept in their daughter's room, but even though the puppy had limited contact with K, it had never shown him hostility. And now it was barking its head off, as if to an intruder, and K was sneezing violently.

And then the inexplicable. As K was trying to get out of range, the puppy dashed underfoot and sank its teeth into his ankle.

K screamed in pain. "Damned dog's gone mad!"

His wife rushed over and checked his leg. The bite mark was streaming blood. MS corralled the puppy and returned it, still yelping frantically, to her room.

"I'm sorry, Daddy. She's usually not touchy like this." She sounded so matter-of-fact about it. "I think she's in heat. We should take her to the vet and get her spayed. Please, don't worry about the bite. You won't get infected, she's had all of her shots."

K felt a sting as his wife applied disinfectant to the wound. After she had dressed it with gauze secured with first-aid tape, K hurried to the bedroom and got dressed. The bite hurt, but he wasn't going to let it put him out of action.

The mutt's hostility juxtaposed with the familiar scene of his wife and daughter on a Saturday morning left K in a deep funk— everyone was against him, everyone was plotting to turn his life upside down. Behind a façade of peace and tranquility they were deceiving him, they were preying on his frailties.

The familiar ring of the alarm clock that morning was somehow different. As was his familiar wife. And his familiar daughter. And the damn puppy was definitely different. His aftershave and his cell phone had up and disappeared to who knows where. There had to be a starting point for these bizarre happenings.

Am I in a shadow box? A shadow box—an experimental visual art form in which layers of paper are manipulated to enhance their three-dimensionality, the silhouette of the multiple strata, viewed at an angle, reinforcing the sense of solidity. Perhaps these enigmatic experiences were happening right now in the three-dimensional space of a shadow box.

9:35 a.m.

Leaves scattered from ginkgo trees like powder from a puff. It was a fine, clear day—autumn didn't get any better than this.

"What a blessing to have nice weather for a wedding," cooed K's wife from the passenger seat.

That's for you to say, thought K. Here he was being dragged to a wedding—what a waste of a beautiful day. MS was in the back seat listening to music through her ear buds. Following his wife's directions, K made a U-turn at an intersection.

Something was very peculiar, unprecedented in fact. When they had left home just now, his wife had shown no signs of her usual obsessions. Normally she spent at least five minutes checking and rechecking the toilet tank, the faucets, the gas stove, the iron, the windows, and finally the door lock. No matter how pressed for time, she felt compelled to perform this routine, and if the routine was out of sequence, she would have to start all over again. K had learned the hard way that if he tried to stop her or made a critical comment, this only made her more anxious. He would end up displeased, annoyed, or angry, but all he could do was remain on the sidelines.

The older she got, the more obsessive she had become. After they had sex she remained on the pot until she'd emptied every last drop.

"She's afraid of getting pregnant," H had once explained. "And of course she connects the semen with that. In effect she's unconsciously blocking the fertilization process. Sometimes we see women who have been sexually abused when they were young wiping down their vagina with a powerful cleanser after sex."

If his wife had been violated, she had never told K about it. But the fact remained that her obsessions had become bad enough for her to undergo those two months of treatment.

But today she was not her usual self. She had taken only a cursory glance at the gas range, the same with the door, and then they had left. Maybe she was in a hurry to get to the hair salon. Still, it was a mystery to K given the seriousness of her condition according to H.

Every crime has leaks and holes, even the "perfect" crime, with its ironclad alibi and absence of fingerprints or clues left behind. With this woman the leaks and holes were critical. She might have thought she had played K's wife down to the last detail, but wearing his pajamas and not exhibiting her obsessive behaviors were tip-offs that she was an impostor.

K had taken a painkiller but still his ankle hurt every time he applied the brakes or hit the gas. *Wretched mutt—what got into it? It wasn't just a coincidence.* Granted, the puppy knew K wasn't fond of it, but pets always knew who the master was. For the puppy to suddenly treat K as a stranger was counterintuitive, it was retrogressive behavior.

They passed through the heart of Kangnam and turned down an alley.

"Here we are," said his wife, giving K an affectionate pat on the shoulder.

Somehow the touch was out of keeping, and it didn't sit well with K, didn't feel quite right. But his wife remained impassive. She and their daughter and the puppy too, they were all the same, pretending nothing was wrong, and now K was feigning the same stolid expression. They'd contaminated him.

"We'll be an hour or so," his wife said, pointing out the place. "Where will you be in the meantime?"

K had a destination in mind but decided to invoke his right to remain silent about it. "I have to check on something" was all he said.

"All right then, take this and I'll call you when we're almost done," she said, handing K her cell phone. "Don't be late. The wedding starts at noon, and we need to be there by eleven-thirty. It's about fifteen minutes from here, so you need to be back by eleven-fifteen at the latest."

"All *right*."

"Ready?" she said to their daughter.

"Bye, Daddy," said MS in her singsong tone.

The hair salon was a one-story structure that had once been a residence. A lone maple stood before it, its foliage aflame. After his wife and daughter had disappeared inside, K parked in the alley and retrieved an object he'd found earlier when he was looking for his cell phone, a matchbox. He wondered how it had ended up in his pocket.

Janus. The name of the establishment, appearing in a fancy design on the matchbox cover. It was no longer common for a bar to give out matchboxes; more often it was a disposable lighter. But this matchbox was a classy item, a collectible even. Janus, the two-faced deity of Roman mythology—he and H must have gone to a place by that name last night. If he wanted his cell phone back, he'd have to go there himself to look for it, since he had no way of contacting H just then. And assuming his wife was correct, he had been in possession of his phone while they were there.

On the matchbox was the phone number. He opened his wife's phone and entered the number. He would wait exactly eleven rings. It had long been his habit to hang up only after an odd number of rings. K wasn't a person driven by compulsion or reliant on superstition. It was just that he considered it basic courtesy to wait at least ten rings before hanging up, which in his case meant eleven rings because he preferred odd to even numbers. There being no answer after the eleventh ring, he ended the call—Janus must be a late-night bar, and probably hadn't opened yet.

Now what? Why not try calling himself again. That way he could leave a second contact number for whoever might have picked up his phone. Because no one would be able to reach him at home now.

One ring, two, three, four... He listened patiently, imagining his phone chirping indistinctly yet plaintively like a cricket in autumn. And where would it be chirping? In a wooded area in the city, on a street with a fire engine wailing, on a stained table in an inn with shuttered windows and faded wallpaper, beneath a shabby bed on which a naked man and woman were entwined.

Finally he heard the automated message: "We're sorry, no one is available to answer your call. After the tone you may connect with voice mail for an additional charge." K thought, then decided. "To leave a message, press one; to page this person, press two." K pressed one. "At the tone, please record your message, then press the star key or the pound key." At the tone K said, "I believe you have my cell phone," trying to sound like a trained voice, to come across as sincere in order to elicit a response. "If you hear this message, I would appreciate it if you called this number." As important as the phone itself was to K, the information it contained was indispensable, and so he added, in an almost pleading tone, "Please respond—I'll make it worth your while."

K pressed the star button and heard the recorded voice instructing him to press two to hear the message he had just sent. Listening to his own familiar voice was embarrassing—he sounded foolish. He snapped the phone shut.

Next he checked the sketch map on the back of the matchbox. Find his way there and he would find his cell phone, or so he hoped. The place was located just across the Han River.

He followed the riverside expressway to the bridge. Crossing the river, he glanced down at the water. It was a rich, deep green, similar in intensity to the colors of the autumn foliage.

At the far end of the bridge he turned left at the Namsan Tunnel and came to a tourist district containing clusters of shops. Tourist buses lined the main thoroughfare, depositing groups of people on the lookout for imitation designer goods. With its throngs of foreign tourists and mixture of signs in Korean and English, the area was Seoul all right, but didn't feel like Seoul. K couldn't understand how an area could look so familiar in the light of day when last night in the taxi it had left no impression in his memory. He must have been possessed.

Turning left at an intersection, K headed uphill and followed the street around a sharp turn. The street narrowed to an alley, and there it was: Janus. He looked for a parking space, but finding none in the cramped alley he simply parked where he was. No worries, he told himself, it would be quick.

The entrance was framed in red. K tested the door. Good—it was open. His mood brightened—he hadn't expected anyone to be there. But as he descended the steps a strange feeling came over him. He definitely didn't remember going downstairs with H last night. What he did remember was a bell sounding as they went inside and a woman welcoming them with a beaming smile and a purring voice. But there was no bell here, and the stairs looked like a mouth about to swallow him. What else could he do but follow them down?

At the bottom of the steps, another door. This one didn't open. No padlock, which meant it must have been locked from inside. The door held a pane of glass that afforded a view of the interior. The lights were on and K noticed a shadow moving about. He rapped on the pane, heard it rattle. Then he heard music, which must have been too loud for whoever was inside to hear him. He knocked again, then discovered a buzzer beside the door. He tried it, and this time the shadow approached from out of the light. The door didn't open, but K heard a woman's voice.

"We're not open yet."

"I know," said K. "But I need to ask about something."

A face appeared in the glass pane to inspect the stranger. K felt a chill—it was a bluish, ghostlike face, puffed and swollen like a drowning victim who has floated to the surface.

"All right, come in," said the voice, and with a dull clunk the door opened.

K stepped inside.

"How can I help you?" said the woman, smoking a cigarette.

She gave every appearance of being a woman, but the voice now sounded like a man's. K could only stare at her. She was gigantic. Everything about her was excessive—her makeup, her revealing clothing, the bulging breasts in their push-up bra.

"I was here last night," said K as he wondered if this woman could possibly have been the spider woman who had glued herself to H in a slow dance last night. "Do you remember me by any chance?"

The woman blew smoke rings while regarding K. K noticed

her red nail polish and imagined a jackal feeding on a corpse then looking up with its blood-stained snout.

"Hmm," she responded, her voice coquettish. "We do have a lot of customers, you know."

When she tittered, K noticed her Adam's apple bobbing.

K looked about. The dance floor he remembered from last night was nowhere to be seen. What he did see was a bar, several stools, and an interior partitioned by curtains into private booths. K sensed he was in a gay bar, a meat rack for satisfying irrepressible but forbidden desires, for individuals desperate to transcend the taboos that prevented them from transgressing sexual identity.

"Uh, last night I had too much to drink and I think I left my cell phone here. Do you keep lost property?"

"Hmm, a cell phone." And now this Janus, with a face that could have been a man's or a woman's, was muttering in a man's voice. He was like a machine that's programmed to alternate between male and female, but his timing was off. "Didn't find anything from last night. Would you care to have a look? Where were you drinking—at the bar or in one of the booths?"

"I, uh, don't really remember," faltered K.

The next thing he knew, Janus had produced a bottle of beer and poured two glasses. Taking a sip from one, she offered the other to K.

"Here you go. Like they say, a boozer needs booze to remember." Again she tittered.

K took a long swallow.

"Is that all?" simpered the woman. "You came just for the cell phone? Nothing else? Such as…?" She sucked on her lip suggestively.

"Janus? Janus?" came a hoarse voice.

K looked about.

"Such as, maybe you're being cute with the cell phone and it's me you wanted to find? Yes, darling? Shall we lock the door?"

Again came the hoarse voice calling twice for Janus.

"Who's that—is there someone else here?" K asked.

"No, don't worry, it's just you and me."

"Janus. Janus."

"Would you like more?"

"I'm good, thank you."

"Janus. Janus."

Janus, thought K. God of two faces, the sun and the moon.

"Shut up!" shouted Janus. "Damned parrot."

K looked to where Janus was shouting. A birdcage hung from the ceiling. Inside it was a parrot, beak open, squawking.

"Janus, Janus!"

K jumped to his feet. "I'm sorry—I have to go."

"What's the rush? Stay a little longer," Janus said, glaring at K.

"No thank you, I just came for my cell phone, that's all."

"Then get the hell out," Janus growled. "And make sure you shut the door."

K did so and climbed the steps back into the light of day. His back was damp with sweat. He saw a black man in a jacket emblazoned with a tiger, heard the man speak in perfect Korean.

"Is this your car?"

"Yes—why?"

"How is anyone supposed to get by?" And then he switched to English: "Son of a bitch."

"I am sorry," K replied in English, and hurried to move the car. What a nightmare. Once again his conscious world felt like a shadow box—optical illusion, delusion, and découpage all in one; a *papertole*, a layered-paper construction that when viewed from a different angle, assumes a different shape and depth of field, a three-dimensional image; a layered cutout. He was sure that Janus was not the place he had visited with H last night, which had a bell above the door and a dance floor. And a dancing woman whose thigh H had been groping through the high cut in her dress. *And a spider woman—was it the same one?—came up and asked in a sultry tone if I wanted to dance and tried to flirt a drink out of me.* That spider woman was not Janus, and Janus, whether a man or a woman, was not the spider woman. In that case, was Janus, the place, that is, part of the hour-and-a-half gap in the filmstrip of his memory? The only way to solve that mystery was to see H. To do that he had to find

H's phone number and call him. And to do that, he had to find his own cell phone.

Back down the alley, he stopped and dug out his wife's cell phone. No messages. *Damn it, I forgot about the security code.* To retrieve voice messages you needed to unlock your phone; no way you could do that without the security code.

What now? Of course—a text message. *Hello. You have my cell phone. Please contact me.* K pressed the Send button, and immediately saw *Sent* come up on the screen. He closed the phone and just as he was about to deposit it in the console, it rang. Instinctively he checked the number. Not recognizing it, he opened the phone.

"Honey?" His wife's voice.

K felt a surge of relief.

"Where are you?"

"Not that far."

"We'll be done in ten minutes. See you soon."

"All right."

At the sound of his wife's voice he felt a burst of energy, like Popeye after a dose of spinach. Off to the hair salon. Perhaps the sight of his wife would free him from the shadow box and its mysteries.

11:35 a.m.

Half an hour before the wedding, people were already swarming about in front of the hotel. K dropped his wife and daughter at the entrance leading up to the wedding hall and proceeded to the underground parking garage. It being the weekend, the garage was at capacity—he had to drop down to the fourth level before he found a space, and just barely.

He inched his way into the tight space and had just opened the door to squeeze out when he noticed the car next to his was rocking. The windows were tinted and he couldn't see inside. Why would an empty car be rocking like that? Pressing his face against the window, he peered inside. A silhouette took shape, filling out to a bare bottom bobbing rhythmically. The bobbing bottom and the rocking car moved in time with the faint moaning of a woman.

K took the elevator to the second floor and the wedding hall, which also doubled as a convention hall. The corridor outside was thronged with guests in formal wear. Floral displays were arrayed along the walls, each bearing the names of the senders.

K found himself heading for the groom's side before he remembered it was his sister-in-law, his wife's sole younger sister, who was getting married, and he changed course. His wife and daughter were receiving the well-wishers who had dropped off their gift money. At the hair salon their freshly made-up faces had looked like masks, and here just outside the wedding hall the effect was even more pronounced—they looked cartoonish, like goblins or ghosts dreaming of becoming human. Beside his wife was his mother-in-law, clad in a *hanbok*. He should have recognized her at first glance, but it took a moment for the realization to dawn.

"Here you are," said the older woman, extending her hands in greeting.

K felt like a fool as he took her hands in his.

"Here you are," came another voice. "Long time no see."

A dignified gentleman next to K's mother-in-law extended a hand. K accepted it, wondering who he was. The voice and the face were familiar but he couldn't immediately place the man.

"Over here, honey," said his wife, taking him by the hand and gesturing beside her. He squeezed in between her and his daughter. One after another K shook hands and exchanged greetings with people he didn't know, as they deposited cash-laden gift envelopes at the greeters' table before proceeding inside. With each hand he shook he asked himself where he knew the person from. He still couldn't place the man next to his mother-in-law, and this bothered him most.

As far as he knew, his mother-in-law was a widow. He took a quick inventory of what his wife had told him: the husband had been a high-ranking government official; he had been involved in a fatal accident, just before K and his wife got married—which was why on their wedding day it was her uncle, her father's younger brother, who had walked her down the aisle.

What's that man doing next to my mother-in-law? K wondered. You would expect that the man standing next to your mother-in-law at a wedding would be her husband. *So she re-married and I didn't know about it? Or—*

"Congratulations."

A pudgy man had taken K's hand and was bowing. K felt a flash of anger at the man's tight grip, but kept his head lowered and managed to mutter a thank-you. He felt uneasy about this masquerade, in which he didn't understand what he was being congratulated for, or why he was expressing his thanks.

Was it possible the man next to his mother-in-law was the uncle who had walked K's wife down the aisle fifteen years ago at their wedding? No, it couldn't be. Hadn't that man passed on as well, last year, from some ailment or other? K clearly remembered attending the funeral with his wife. Hadn't she wept aloud at the memory of her uncle standing in for her father at the wedding? *The next thing you're going to tell me*, K scolded himself, *he's back from the dead just for the wedding*.

It was too warm. Perspiration streamed down K's face. He kept mopping himself with his handkerchief, but that didn't prevent fatigue from settling in.

More guests had lined up at the groom's table than on the bride's side. The lines were so long you might have thought admission tickets were necessary and the two sides were competing to see who could sell more of them. The groom had just offered a formal greeting to the bridal party and was now back beside his parents, stiff as a soldier in full dress uniform being reviewed by a visiting dignitary. K knew nothing about the man, not his name, where he lived, or what he did for a living. K was bothered by his smugness, the way the man greeted him and shook his hand with delight just because of their connection through his sister-in-law. *The guy must be an actor—either that or he's been married half a dozen times already*.

"I've heard a lot about you," he said during their handshake, his head still bowed.

Lying sack of... What good reason would his sister-in-law have had to talk at length about him? After all, he himself knew little about his sister-in-law, and never talked about her. Fat chance of her gabbing about him.

From inside the wedding hall came a clamorous fanfare and an announcement: "The ceremony is about to commence. Will the parents of the bride and groom please enter, followed by the other guests." K jumped at the opportunity, found his designated place—directly behind the bride's parents—and sat.

K glanced at the images, projected onto a large screen against the back wall, of the soon-to-be bride and groom, then watched as his mother-in-law took her place in front of him, followed by the mystery man. The man's hair, dyed blacker than black, and his wrinkled face made him look like a prune. His white dentures, appearing whenever he laughed, intensified the contrast.

"That man," K ventured to his wife, "who is he, anyway?"

She inspected her mask-like face one last time in her compact.

"Which man?"

"The one next to your mom."

"Don't tell me you don't recognize your own father-in-law, my dad?"

K swallowed heavily. And then Dad, alias Father-in-Law, rose to play the role of walking the bride down the aisle. K scrutinized the man. He still didn't recognize him, but he was most certainly not K's father-in-law, his wife's dad. As far as he knew, his wife's dad had died. *How can a man who died fifteen years ago resurrect himself for his daughter's wedding?*

The wedding proceeded in spite of K's misgivings.

The officiant came to the podium. He wore the usual white gloves and reminded K of an auctioneer. Off to the side, the master of ceremonies announced that the wedding would now begin. *What a clown!* thought K. Taking his cue, the toy soldier groom, complete with his been-there-done-that smugness, marched down the aisle and came to a stop before the podium. And then to the drone of the wedding march, in came the Barbie doll bride in her white, paper-thin dress, wearing an I'm-so-happy-I-could-die smile, hand in hand with her reanimated father, the spirit-ghost. All the colored lights in the hall focused on her, and with the artificial mist the scene resembled a tawdry night club act.

Tears streamed nonstop from his overwrought wife's eyes, while his corpulent mother-in-law's body heaved with sobs. As soon as the bride arrived at the podium, the groom took her like a relay runner completing a baton hand-off. The mysterious imposter flashed a doting, toothy smile and relinquished the bride. K could almost hear him saying *I know you'll look after her.* And then the man returned to his place and plopped himself down, weary but contented, a sprinter who has broken the finish-line tape.

From then on it was full speed ahead. Wedding rings and marriage vows were exchanged. "Will you love her for better or for worse, through illness and good health?" To K's ears it sounded like, *You had better… or else.* The groom answered with a resounding "I will!" It was less a pledge of love to his bride and more a comedian's quip to draw laughter from the guests. And sure enough, the assemblage obliged him. In contrast, the bride's "I will" could barely be heard.

The master of ceremonies then introduced the "honored professor," the officiant in his white gloves, who proceeded to make the wedding hall into his very own lecture hall. He began by outlining marriage as a social responsibility and moved on slowly and surely to the post-family-breakdown couples of the future. K found the lecture tedious and began to nod off. He tried to forestall sleep with a drink of water and then a soft drink from the courtesy table nearby, but it was no use—he ended up falling asleep. The next thing he knew, someone was shaking him awake. How long had he been out?

His wife was scowling at him. "How can you sleep at a time like this?"

White Gloves was still going strong. In an emphatic tone that seemed to herald the ending of his speech, he said that in Russia there is a proverb: pray once before you go to war, pray twice before you go out to sea, pray three times before you get married. "But," he urged the couple, "over the course of your marriage you should pray thousands of times and not just three." This finale managed to impress the guests, bored as they were, and they bobbed their heads.

K, meanwhile, was losing his battle with the forces of sleep, and in spite of his wife's admonition he dropped off again. This time he had a dream. He was driving on an expressway. The brakes wouldn't obey him and the car began to skid down a slope. K was frightened awake. The lecture had finally ended and the bride and groom were formally greeting the parents on both sides. K's mother-in-law remained seated, dabbing at her eyes with a handkerchief, while the mystery man played to a T the role of father-of-the-bride by rising to his feet to accept the greeting.

Where did this guy pop up from? Had the family picked him up at a last-call actors guild? Or had the father managed to resuscitate himself for a curtain call? For sure the guy must be an actor. The only other possibility was that his mother-in-law had remarried. She certainly had the wherewithal.

K was well aware of his mother-in-law's reputation as a floozy. She was also a loan shark and had accumulated a pile of money. Enough to have a den of gigolos at her beck and call. One of her pastimes, in fact, was to stash away a couple of these young lounge lizards on her trips to the hot springs. His wife explained away her mother's gigolo fixation as the one and only stress reliever for a lonely woman without a husband. But K did not discount the possibility that her huge assets might also be a factor. She neither liked nor trusted K, and K knew it. He didn't like her either. The sight of her always called to mind the Maupassant story "Boule de Suif."

K also knew that from early on his mother-in-law had tried to provoke his wife into divorcing him. Why get married and bore yourself to tears when you can stay single and enjoy life? Such was the tune she always whistled.

Which led K back to the body double posing as her husband. He didn't fit the young-playmate profile. Didn't that mean she had settled on a more age-appropriate dance partner, selecting him as carefully as she managed her money-lending operation?

The ceremony ended and the bride and groom made their exit. The banquet followed in short order. The menu was steak. K was hungry, but the meat was leathery and bland and after a few bites he started gagging. He slipped away to the men's room and retched once in the toilet. As he washed his hands he remembered having put his wife's cell phone on silent before the wedding. He produced the phone and checked the screen. Sure enough—*One missed call.* And there was his cell phone number. It had to be the person who had recovered his phone.

K punched in the number, heard the rings trembling in his ear.

"Hello." A man's voice. K didn't recognize it.

"Hello," said K. "This is the owner of the cell phone you're using."

"Ah yes," said the voice. "I tried to call just now but no one answered."

"I'm sorry, I wasn't able to take it just then," K responded, feeling like it was somehow his fault.

"Not at all. How can I return your phone?"

"If it's all right, we could meet this afternoon."

"Works for me—it's the weekend. Would you mind if we met over this way?"

"Over this way" meant a modest apartment complex in the Chamshil area. K agreed to meet him at 2:30 in a commercial district nearby.

"I'll be wearing a red hiking cap," said the man.

"All right," said K.

He emerged from the men's room; he didn't really want to return to the banquet, but he had to return his wife's cell phone. He found her and their daughter avidly dicing their steak and eating with obvious pleasure. The bride and groom had changed out of their wedding finery and were going from table to table greeting the guests. Perfunctory cheering and clapping erupted from here and there.

"Are you all right?" his wife said through a mouthful of steak.

"I went to the men's room—I was a little queasy."

"Then why don't you leave first? We have to stay for the *p'yebaek,* then drop by my mom's on the way home."

"All right—I just got in touch with the man who has my cell phone and we're going to meet."

"Well. You really are useless—make sure your head's screwed on tight so you don't lose that too."

K returned her cell phone. "Something I wanted to ask," K said, lowering his voice and trying to soften his tone. "Who *is* that man?"

"What man?" his wife said, trying to saw through a gristly chunk of meat.

"That one, sitting next to your mother."

The man seemed enraptured by his wine.

"I told you—it's my dad," she snapped.

"Your *dad*? But you said he died just before we got married."

"Well." His wife looked at him with a straight face. "Well, I didn't want it known that I come from a broken family. I'd rather be thought of as the daughter of a widow than the daughter of a divorcée."

"You mean he didn't die in an accident?"

"They got divorced—that's why I said what I said."

"Then..." K still didn't understand. "If they're divorced, why is he there beside her?"

"*Someone* had to walk the bride down the aisle. And my uncle died, remember? So today is a onetime thing." His wife looked so nonchalant. "They're a couple for today only. After the ceremony he goes back to his home and Mom goes back to hers."

K was stunned. He silently drank a soda. So Dad returns to his wife and children and Mom returns to her slave gallery, their hours-long joint performance a perfect crime. A masquerade that ends with husband and wife removing their masks and returning to their homes. Like pickpockets returning to their den after lightening the pockets of their victims. Like vampires returning to their coffins after sucking at their victims' necks. The man and woman masquerading as bride and groom, their marriage legalized, setting off on their honeymoon and having legalized sex in a hotel room. The bride performing her role of virgin, the groom performing his role of superstud.

"Can you stay long enough for the family photos?" said his wife meekly.

Back in the wedding hall the bride and groom were being photographed with White Gloves, who had wedged himself between the couple, a notary certifying the legality of the marriage.

There was a burst of camera flashes, followed by an announcement from the master of ceremonies:

"Will the families of the bride and groom please come forward."

"Let's go," said K's wife. K and their daughter followed her to the stage and took their places on the bride's side. K's mother-in law and her erstwhile mate, now a stranger but playing to perfection the role of husband, sauntered up and stood next to the bride. Again the role-playing father-in-law extended a hand in greeting to K.

"I've heard a lot about you, young fella."

K took the man's hand and bowed.

"I appreciate the fact you've done right by my daughter—good to know you can trust a man."

K wasn't sure how to respond to being buttered up, but realized he had to say something. "Well," he murmured, "a man has to do the right thing."

"Lookie here, my little granddaughter," the grandfather mask said, cupping the girl's cheeks.

"Hello, Grandfather," said the daughter mask in her sing-song voice.

The two families were now gathered together, an assembly of strangers, like a ragtag group of reservists thrown together on a training ground. They were joined by bonds of blood but displayed no intimacy, radiated no warmth. K felt like one of a band of con men posing as a family.

"All eyes on the camera, please. At the far right in back, a little closer in, please."

The photographer maneuvered the group with the ease of a sergeant drilling his reservists. Once again K was sweating and once again he produced his handkerchief and wiped his face. He felt like a carton of milk that's past its shelf life, window dressing in the dairy section of a supermarket named Family, with his wife in the Wife aisle, his father-in-law in the Father-of-the-Bride corner, and his sister-in-law a new product sample. And there they all stood.

"Smile," commanded the photographer like a trainer who finally has his dogs under control. He held high the cord attached to the shutter. "All right, *kimchi*."

Before he knew it K had mumbled *"kimchi."* His blind obedience annoyed him.

"I'm going," K said once they were back at their table.

"All right. Like I said, after the *p'yebaek* we're dropping by my mom's—we'll be home around dinnertime."

That's right, thought K. It was the final act in this farce. The *p'yebaek*—the bride and groom in their *hanbok* bowing to both sets of parents.

"Daddy's leaving," he said to his daughter.

"Bye, Daddy," she said in her singsong voice, sounding like a doll that speaks when you press the button in its belly.

Outside the wedding hall K felt liberated. As the elevator lowered him to the parking garage he wondered about the couple having sex. The two cars were so close together he was afraid of bumping their door with his, and he didn't want to disturb their afternoon delight. Outside the elevator he noticed the car was still in motion, rocking like a cradle soothing a cranky child at bedtime. Reluctantly he pressed the unlock button on his keyless and while opening the door looked inside the other car. As before, the tinted windows revealed only the faint silhouettes of two bodies bobbing gently like seaweed on the tide.

He noticed a flyer behind his windshield wiper and snatched it before climbing inside. *Damned nuisance.* He glanced at the flyer: <u>Liver and Kidneys</u>. *Must be from a butcher shop nearby.* K imagined a restaurant specializing in various cuts of meat: sirloin strips, rib strips, flank strips, short ribs, liver, kidney, tripe, minced beef, intestine. And then he turned the flyer over: <u>Liver, Kidneys, All Organs for Sale; Wanted—Healthy Livers, Kidneys, Eyes; Please Contact...</u> And at the bottom of the flyer, <u>Your Precious Offering Can Save a Life.</u> So—an ad from a purveyor of human organs.

And so, K thought as he exited the parking garage, perhaps what he had assumed to be sex in the adjoining car was actually an illegal surgery, the extraction of a liver or kidney from a living body—an organ smuggler at work in an illicit slaughterhouse.

K thought he smelled a bloody stink. He gagged, then clenched his teeth.

He emerged into blinding light. The trick wedding, the disgusting back-seat sex, the unseemly commerce in human organs—a bombed-out battlefield bathed by the scintillating autumn sun.

2:23 p.m.

The sidewalks were clogged with baseball fans headed for the nearby stadium. The younger ones wore team jerseys and chanted, and the fans of each team kept to their side of the street. K heard a chant from one of the processions: "No, no, our team's the best. Yes, yes, we've got the zest. Day game, night game, we're the best." Skittering along behind those fans were young women outfitted in short skirts and trailing clusters of festive balloons. There were fathers bearing children on their shoulders. K seemed to be the only one going against the tide.

He caught sight of the place where he'd arranged to meet the man with his cell phone. The Chamshil area that K remembered was pretty much a wasteland, but now it boasted an array of shops and high-rise apartment buildings—a new urban center south of the Han River, the "new town."

K had arrived in plenty of time to find a parking garage—so far so good. The café mentioned by the man—a place offering a simple meal and coffee—was a sunny ground-floor location with a young clientele. Most of the tables were next to the windows, the occupants sipping coffee and watching the world go by.

K searched for the red cap, didn't see it, and decided to sit. All he'd had for breakfast was a slice of toast, a few diced vegetables, a sip of milk, and coffee. And he'd pretty much skipped lunch, managing only a couple of chunks of steak at the wedding banquet before feeling sick to his stomach. But hungry though he was, he wasn't ready for solid food. Instead he ordered a latte.

As he returned to his seat he felt a stab of pain in his ankle. *Of all the shit luck.*

He rolled up his pants leg. The bite was an angry red. The latte had the bitter taste of coffee that's not fresh. K began to worry—what if he caught rabies and turned into a mad dog himself? He looked at his glass of water. *Let's do a little hydrophobia test just to make sure.* He took a drink. No problem. He could breathe easy now.

His gaze came to rest on the next table. A woman sat there, checking her watch. And then she checked it again. Waiting for someone? No, K told himself, she was just killing time. She wore a trench coat, which was unbuttoned to reveal a black dress, and sat with her legs crossed and thighs visible. K was not a voyeur, but the woman's table was right in front of him with nothing to block his view. She must have been aware of K's gaze, because she occasionally pulled down the hem of the dress. But each time she did this, the higher it rode back up. Maybe she was enjoying his gaze, and trying to tempt him? She was doing something with her cell phone, but maybe it was just a pretense. Good thing she was wearing sunglasses—K could avoid eye contact.

He considered changing tables. Not that he was discomfited—it was just that he didn't want her thinking he was responding to her provocative pose. K would be the first to tell you he didn't have a leg fetish, he wasn't a dirty old man who yielded to the slightest temptation. Rather, he thought of the female body as being like a can of coffee or soda dropping out of a vending machine. With the lone exception of his wife's body.

But he remained where he was. Moving meant disclosing his awareness of the woman's presence; the smart thing to do was simply enjoy the scenery. *Who knows, maybe she'll move instead.* K kept his gaze squarely on the woman.

And then a man appeared and sat down across from her. The man's head and broad shoulders partially blocked the woman from view. But then she stripped off her coat. *That's more like it.* Followed by her sunglasses.

I've seen that face. But where? In a TV drama? The movies? And then he knew. Her face looked like something out of an "after" photo of a woman who had run the gamut of plastic surgery to achieve the prevailing standard of beauty—Botox injections, eyelid enlargement, nose job, chin surgery, tooth implants. External counterparts to the "healthy" internal organs advertised in the flyer left on K's windshield. K imagined this woman's face adorning a flyer for a plastic surgery clinic.

K thought he understood why she had removed her sunglasses. Until then she had been the coy woman, aware of K's gaze and yet masking her flirtatious enticements, but now that the man was here, she could strip the pretense and look the stranger in the eye with naked brazenness. She kept one eye on the man across from her and with the other looked straight at K, taking delight in her visual fornication with him. And just to make sure K got the message she uncrossed her legs and spread them inch by inch. If men's exhibitionism was a proud display of surging manhood, then women's was a modest display of subtle womanhood, just enough cleavage revealed to draw the viewer to the edge. But this woman was enjoying herself by exposing genitalia like men, drawing attention to what lay between her spreading legs. What with the backlighting of the sun coming through the window behind her, the white of her inner thighs made the shadowed recess within look like a tunnel, a black hole that would suck everything in. K observed that pit with no feeling of arousal, like a biologist peering into a microscope. The woman heaved a great yawn. To K that yawn was her libido at work, a tiny flash point of her heat.

K felt manipulated—there was no fun in this. He rose to find a different table and spotted a man in a red cap at a table near the serving counter. Latte in hand, K approached the man.

"Hello. Are you the person I spoke with?"

The man was midway through a plate of spaghetti.

"Th—that's right," the man hastened to reply before doffing his cap.

He might just as well have kept it on, K thought, considering the sorry display that was revealed—a few long seaweed-like strands of hair transplanted in a bare runway.

"Thanks very much for hanging on to my phone," said K. "I appreciate it."

The man was grossly cross-eyed. His eyes were looking in different directions, refusing to cooperate with each other, and K couldn't figure out which eye was focusing on him. And so he went back and forth between them, making sure neither was receiving short shrift during their conversation. *But what if he isn't an equal opportunity sort of guy?* K decided instead to focus on a point midway between his eyes.

As he chewed spaghetti the man reached into his pocket and produced a cell phone. Sure enough it was K's. But instead of returning it to K he stroked it absently.

"You must have been in a tizzy without it," said the man. "Don't get me wrong, I wasn't snooping, but I wanted to find out who it belonged to, and I noticed a lot of information. I can see that you'd be in a fix without it."

"Th—that's right," said K. He noticed the man's nose was puffy and red like his own ankle. He must have been a heavy drinker.

"I know you tried to reach me a couple of times," said the man. "But this morning I slept in. I knew there was a voice message, but I couldn't access it without the security code. And then I got your text message and that's when I knew you were looking for your phone. That's what people do—unless they say what the hell and give up. It's kind of like a criminal going back to the crime scene to make sure he didn't leave anything behind." The man laughed.

It was a clumsy attempt at humor, comparing K to a criminal, but he went along with it and forced a hearty laugh.

The man gauged K's response, still stroking the phone. "You need to be careful, sir." The man's smile broadened until his face became a caricature. "When I was trying to figure out who owned it I came across a real toe-curler of a video clip," the man chuckled. His cross eyes seemed amused.

K looked at the right eye; it was laughing. He looked at the left eye; it was sneering.

"I thought about getting rid of it, but that's not my prerogative now, is it. But you need to be careful, sir. It's too naughty for a gentleman like yourself."

Damned if I know what you're talking about. But you're the boss. And with this thought K nodded meekly. "I appreciate it..."

Would the man ever hand over his phone? "How can I make it up to you?"

"Oh, don't mention it," said the man. His right eye was still laughing, but now the left eye was cunning and calculating. "It's the right thing to do, returning a lost item to its owner." He continued to stroke the phone, then flipped it open and closed it. "Especially with that clip," he said helpfully. "We don't want anyone else knowing about it now, do we."

"But still," said K, "I know it's a chore—nobody has time to do lost-and-found for others. It must be a headache for you."

The man's right eye was still laughing, but the left eye had turned serious.

"To be honest, it is a bit of a nuisance. At first I didn't want to get involved—let someone else figure out whether to return it or keep it, it was none of my concern. And for all I knew, the owner might come looking for it. But when no one showed up for an hour and a half, I thought I ought to hang onto it."

"An hour and a half?"

"That's right."

"Where the heck did you find it anyway?"

"What!" Both of the cross-eyes shot K a hard look. "You don't know where you left it?"

K sipped his latte, cold by now. There was a long silence.

"Tell you what," said the man, "do you have a minute?"

"Of course," said K.

"All right. I'm an insurance planner. Life insurance, mainly. What would you say to taking out a policy? Cancer insurance is popular these days. Did you know cancer affects one out of every three men, one out of four women? It's a psychological shock for sure, but there's also a tremendous financial impact—the cost of treatment is astronomical."

K felt like he was listening to a recording.

"For a measly 14,000 *won* monthly premium, you get a 20 million lump sum if you're diagnosed. And that premium is not going to go up."

"All right, I'll take it," said K, wanting to cut short the man's spiel. He was tired. The man's right eye was apologetic but his left eye was triumphant. He produced a contract from a briefcase. "Shall we go over the policy?"

"No need. You and I both know who the actual beneficiary is here."

"Good thinking. But to be honest, cancer insurance isn't a moneymaker for us. I wouldn't be surprised if we stop offering it before too long. With cancer insurance it's party A that benefits more than party B."

"And I am...," said K.

"Party A, of course."

K signed the document and wrote down his bank account number for auto-payment of the premium.

Party B presented a copy of the signed policy to K. "Now don't get me wrong, this isn't why I came here," he said with a sheepish expression.

"No worries," said party A. And no sooner had he pocketed the policy than the cell phone was back in K's hand.

"Aren't you going to make sure it's yours?" said party B.

"It's mine all right," said party A after a quick inspection showed his wife and daughter on the screen. "Thank you."

"All right, then, if there's nothing else—" said party B.

"Wait—where did you find it? I was rather the worse for wear, don't have the foggiest notion where I was."

"In a movie theater," said party B. "Had myself a late dinner and a movie—Friday night, you know. It was in the seat pocket in front of me. Thought about turning it in, but when the movie was over and no one came for it, I decided I'd hold on to it."

"Movie theater? Where?"

"Up on the third floor. Let's see." Party B ferreted through his pockets. "Ah, here it is," he said, displaying a ticket stub.

"Could I see it?' said party A.

"You can *have* it—it's no use to me." And with that, party B rose, anxious to depart lest party A change his mind about the policy. "I'll be on my way. Oh, I got hungry while I was waiting—hope you don't mind taking care of the bill." And then he was gone.

Party A examined the stub, noted the seat number. How in the name of Orson Welles/Alfred Hitchcock/Im Kwŏn-t'aek had his cell phone ended up in a seat pocket in a movie theater? He never went to the movies, couldn't remember the last time he'd set foot in a theater. The artificial settings, the unnatural antics of the players, the contrived productions—no thank you. During that one-and-a-half-hour gap in the filmstrip of his memory, could he have gone to an unfamiliar theater to watch an unfamiliar movie and gone home without his cell phone? No way! Not in that time frame. Maybe with Superman's speed; otherwise it would take a miracle.

If, in fact, he and H had taken a taxi north across the Han River to some drinking den last night, it would have taken a good hour to get from there to where he was now. And even if he spent only a few minutes in the theater and had gone straight home, it would be a matter of hours from north of the Han to home and bed. Leaving his cell phone in that theater—the logistics just didn't play out.

What if a thief had dumped his cell phone in this unfamiliar theater like a heartless mother abandoning her baby? K thought of the nurse at H's clinic. She was perfectly capable of something like that. Maybe she'd wanted to make an ass of K—pilfering the phone while they ate, killing time watching the movie, leaving it in the seat pocket. But that was a stretch. Hadn't his wife sworn that around ten she'd called him and he'd said he would soon be home from the bar?

He opened the phone and checked the call log, working his way back from the most recent calls to last night. The three most recent calls had come from their home phone and his wife's cell phone—consistent with the fact that that morning he had made three phone calls, in addition to leaving the voice message and sending the text message. No discrepancy there—K's memory served him correctly.

So, back to last night's calls. As best he remembered, it was around seven that he had called H from in front of the clinic. And then around ten, or so he was told, he had gotten the call from his wife. Sure enough, those were the only two calls appearing in the log. The cell phone chip and his brain were working in tandem.

The last sent call was 7:13. The incoming call from his wife was 10:14. He touched the screen where their home phone number appeared. Strangely enough, "Missed call" came up, along with the missed-call tone.

Missed call? That meant K hadn't answered. But that morning his wife had clearly stated she had spoken with him on the phone around 10 p.m. So how did the missed call fit in? Someone else must have talked with his wife and told her he would return home soon. But who? Someone wasn't telling the truth. Was it K himself? His wife? Party B? The cell phone? Did yesterday get confused? Today? Was the movie theater lying? The bar?

K didn't know what was what.

Well, why not go up to the third floor and see if the movie theater was indeed there? He got up, ticket stub in hand.

3:31 p.m.

The theater had three screens. The ticket stub was for number 3. Playing there was a movie K had never heard of, *City of the Blind.* The 2:30 show had started, with the next screening scheduled for 4:30. He checked the time of the last showing—10:30. Party B had said he'd gone to the late show, which meant K's cell phone had been left there before that time.

"One for *City of the Blind*, please." K paid the cashier.

"The next showing starts in about 50 minutes. Are you okay with that, sir?"

K nodded—what else could he do? Out came a ticket like a tongue from a mouth.

K found a seat in the lounge, which bustled with young people enjoying their Saturday afternoon. They were munching on popcorn, sucking on soda, and chattering away, friends, boyfriends, girlfriends. K seemed to be the oldest person there. He noticed that the other two theaters were showing Korean films. He had a hunch that most everyone was waiting for those two, that few were there to see *City of the Blind.* K read the poster: *Based on the novel by Nobel Prize-winning Portuguese author José Saramago.*

So what if he won the Nobel Prize? So what if the film won a jury award? City of the Blind. What kind of title was *that*? It reeked of the artiste, the issue-oriented auteur. Even if he was on autopilot last night, why would he want to watch a film with such a creepy title? Besides, it had been an age since he'd seen *any* movie anywhere.

The lounge was too crowded, so upstairs K went to the waiting area outside theater 3. The few viewers he saw there reeked of the snootiness of patrons of the arts who look down their noses at anything less than a masterpiece. K had a look at the seating chart posted on the wall, then checked party B's ticket stub. C45. C meant a row near the front, 45 was on the far left.

He checked his watch. 45 minutes left. He didn't have time to waste. He approached the usher, a young woman who seemed bored to tears and was knitting.

"Sorry, but could you let me in? I don't have a lot of time."

The usher unstrapped the cord.

"Try not to disturb the other guests. And it's dark, so you can grab any empty seat."

It was indeed dark inside, but soon K understood why she had been so agreeable. There were virtually no spectators, hardly anyone to disturb by entering midway through the show. What an embarrassment! He waited for his eyes to adjust before groping his way toward the area he had scouted out on the seating map. Finding the central aisle, he made his way to row C and turned left. As he felt his way along he touched someone. A man, and there a woman, and they were in a strange position—were they having sex? They must not have been here for the movie, either. They probably wanted a dark compartment, closed off from the broad light of day, to satisfy their urges, and had chosen an artsy-fartsy film that wouldn't attract many viewers. The location wasn't important. The seats might as well have been drawn in a lottery—A24, B17, F31, it didn't matter as long as the surroundings were dark and the ambience hidden. They were like drug addicts seeking a place to inject the poison of artificial pleasure—a public toilet, an alley, a fire escape, a rooftop, seat H15, seat J23. Or like gay men looking for a place to plant themselves in each other's rosy sphincters—the murky nook of a theater, a dumpster, seat A13, seat F43, anywhere they could satisfy their lust.

There, C45. Unoccupied. K sat. By now his eyes had fully adjusted, and with the light reflected from the screen he could inspect the interior of the theater. He saw no more than half a dozen spectators, none in his immediate vicinity.

The first thing he did was check the seat pocket in front of him. Empty. He placed his cell phone in it, removed it, repeated the sequence. This was the very seat, the very pocket where his cell phone was found. But K hadn't been here. Couldn't have been here. And yet this was where the phone had been found. During that one-and-a-half-hour gap in K's consciousness a shadow person had left a trace of K, then disappeared. But why here, in this seat pocket?

Perplexed, K gazed at the screen. Before long he was able to put together a rough outline of the story. One ordinary day, a driver waiting at a stoplight suddenly loses his vision. And then so does his eye doctor, and then an entire hospital ward, and then the general public. Panic breaks out. The government declares that an infectious disease is to blame, and proceeds to quarantine the blind. The hospital ward becomes a living hell—the only person there who can still see is the eye doctor's wife. She observes soldiers ruthlessly killing the blind for fear they'll be infected, and she witnesses them raping women. And then the ward catches fire, the soldiers guarding it run off, and the quarantined patients escape.

The story was as creepy to K as the title. But whereas the viewers might fear they themselves were contaminated, that their sight was washed out, K was afraid that his memory was washed out.

At this point in the film, those who had fled the ward with the help of the doctor's wife, the only surviving sighted person, were wandering the streets in search of food. In this hell-on-earth city they relieved themselves anywhere they could. They encountered starving dogs feeding on the corpses of the dead. It was a particularly gruesome scene, but K could hear chuckles. And then the victims found a grocery story, which they frantically looted. This scene drew suppressed laughter from the audience that sounded to K like farting—the handful of viewers unable to contain their laughter but reluctant to be heard laughing out loud.

K didn't know what to make of it—what did the half-dozen moviegoers find so funny about that scene? Were there comic elements to it, or jokes they found amusing? No, it couldn't be—those same viewers had chuckled when the dogs were ripping and gnawing at the corpses of the humans. How could they all laugh at that cruel scene? Had they come down with a "laugh-out-loud virus" in the same way that those in the movie were infected by the blindness disease?

K felt alienated. *Why me?* He felt as isolated from the others in the theater (few though they were) as the doctor's wife did from the blind around her.

When was the last time he'd had a good laugh, anyway? He thought about the reality of his life and wondered if he had ever had a good laugh in any of its scenes. He pored over his memories but nothing came to mind. He heard another chorus of soft, fart-like chuckling, the viewers this time laughing at a chaotic scene in which the doctor's wife was ushering the survivors into her home. To dispel his feeling of alienation K forced himself to laugh along with the others, until his shoulders shook with the effort. But it was empty laughter, air leaking from a balloon.

He had forgotten how to laugh. Whatever had happened to the eyesight of the people in the movie, K's sense of humor appeared to have suffered the same fate

How could I forget how to laugh? Again he searched his memory. *When was the last time I laughed?*

From the recesses of his memory an anecdote came to mind. Early in grade school, was it? He was reading a children's magazine, and something he saw had made him laugh out loud.

One day Little Smarty doesn't want to go to school. He comes up with a clever idea. He calls his homeroom teacher.

"Is this Little Smarty's homeroom teacher? Our Little Smarty isn't feeling well and can't come to school today."

"Excuse me, but could you tell me who is calling?"

"Uh, well, sir, it's my father."

It's my father. Young K found it hilarious. He told the story to everyone he met, but the only person who had ever laughed was his mother. "Funniest thing I ever did hear," she would say, patting her young son affectionately on the back. And now he realized he was smiling the smile that came just before he would burst into laughter, the laughter that would explode at any moment like a sneeze he was trying to hold back.

Well, it's my father, sir.

And finally he chuckled. It wasn't that he'd forgotten how to laugh; rather, he'd lost all opportunity. But was that the only time he had laughed? He canvassed his memory one last time, but nothing came up. Did the survival in his memory of only this one short episode mean that his wellspring of laughter was now arid as a desert?

The movie was approaching a climax. The people the doctor's wife had brought home now had food and shelter. And then one day, one of the afflicted men suddenly regained his sight. Oh, the colors with which his vision was flooded. The others too regained their ability to see, albeit more gradually.

The ending was so emotional. K couldn't see the expressions of the others, but knew instinctively that once the pathos of the story had sunk in, any sensitive viewer would cry.

And then the flip side of the question came to mind. Had he ever burst into tears? This memory search was similarly unproductive. Had he lost all opportunity to cry too? Like the people in the movie with the blindness disease, had a virus deprived K of his ability to cry?

Well, there *was* that one time, also early in grade school and also connected with something he had read. As best he could remember, it was *The Adventures of Tom Sawyer*. He tried to recall the main strands of the narrative. Tom Sawyer, along with Huckleberry Finn, was giving his poor aunt a hard time—now what was her name, Polly, Lily, Elizabeth? Polly, maybe. The boys liked to play together, getting into mischief and making a racket, and one day his Aunt Polly told Tom in exasperation to go jump in the Mississippi River. Yes, that's how it had happened. Tom had tried to imagine his aunt wailing at the sight of his drowned self. "Dear God, how could you do this? Yes, my Tom could be a scamp, but he was also my little angel, very polite to me, and such a brave boy."

Young K had begun bawling at this scene. From then on, whenever he recalled it, the tears flowed. He could identify with Tom imagining his own death. And if he were to throw himself into the Han River, his mother too would have made a tearful appeal—she was a devout Catholic and it was owing to her influence that K still went to church. *Dear God, my little K was so sweet, he wouldn't lie if his life depended on it, such a handsome boy, he meant so much to me.*

K knew better—he had not been a good boy. But the K of his imagination *was* a good boy. Nor in reality was he good-looking or dependable. But the boy of his imagination was as noble as a little prince. K's tears were merely a matter of wallowing in self-pity. He hadn't cried his last year in grade school when his father was hit by a car and killed. He didn't like his alcoholic father, and whenever he witnessed him battering his mother, he prayed that God would make him go away. And when this powerful being answered his prayer, part of him felt relief.

The best cry K had ever had was when his mother passed away. At the time, he was completing his military service. She was the only person to share his feelings, laughing when he laughed, crying when he cried. K was at her bedside when she breathed her last.

"K, dear, come on now, get down from that ladder," she had said.

What ladder? He had never been up a ladder before. And then she had taken one last breath and was gone.

"*Aigo, aigo!*" his older sister had wailed. "Mom, Mom!"

And K had followed suit. He cried not so much from sorrow as from losing a favorite toy, a treasure.

Whenever K had been anxious his mother had told him, "Don't worry—just let the worry doll take care of it." The worry doll was how his mother referred to God. And her death was to K like the loss of his one and only worry doll. When he worried, she had taken on his worries. The loss of the worry doll had been utter terror for K.

And now, here in the theater, he couldn't even recall her face.

"Mother," he groaned. The moment he said it, he felt tears—the glands producing transparent fluid and filling the tear ducts to the release point with the slightly salty moisture. But the amount was too tiny to flow and in no time had dried up.

The film was over except for the credits. The lights came on and the viewers perked up like field mice hiding in the dark. The couple K had brushed past earlier were gazing wistfully at the credits, like creatures that have finished mating.

K remained where he was. He was curious about the half of the movie he'd missed, but there was also the nagging question left by his encounter with party B, and he had the ten-minute break until the next screening to find an answer. *When I was trying to figure out who owned it, I came across a real toe-curler of a video clip... It's too naughty for a gentleman like yourself.*

Too naughty—what the hell was that supposed to mean? He opened the phone and examined it. Everything was there, the crucial information about his business contacts and his wife and daughter. Next he pressed "my pictures." He still wasn't used to taking photos and video clips, or retrieving them. Photos appeared on the screen. Photos taken by his daughter. The majority were shots of the backyard of the rectory, taken after Mass one day last spring when the cherry trees were in full bloom. He checked each of the photos. Most were of his wife (a few graced by K as well), her radiant smile coming off as a dowdy smirk against the sumptuous cherry blossoms.

There were shots of the puppy as well. The images revived the pain in his ankle.

Next he pressed "go to video." The screen was briefly blank, then suddenly an image of jolting movement. At first he didn't know what it was, only something flesh-colored and bobbing, unfocused, looking like an overblown close-up of fruit. But soon he realized, as he had in the parking garage, that he was seeing a pair of buttocks. No, indeed, not the sort of thing to be stored in a cell phone.

It was an embarrassment all right. A naked man and woman on a bed having sex, and nothing coy about it. The woman's privates were in view, and aiming toward them the man's erect penis. Even more embarrassing was the audio. K thought at first the woman was moaning, then realized she was cursing. And then whoever was shooting shifted the focus, a *Check this out* cue, to a close-up of the woman's face. And that was it, about ten seconds in all.

K couldn't believe his eyes. The face was familiar—it was none other than that of his wife. But more than shock it was irritation he felt. *How vulgar!* It was obviously his wife having sex on that bed. But the setting wasn't their bedroom—the curtains were wrong, the objects unfamiliar. And who was his wife having sex with? Was that heaving bottom *his?* Were those curses, that yowling of a cat in heat really *hers?*

Or was his wife fornicating—was she with another man, in another place, transformed into a different woman? And how did this clip get into his phone? Had someone caught his wife having an affair? If so, the prime suspect would be party B. And the motive—to get K's attention?

Just then the phone vibrated. K checked the screen, saw his wife's cell phone number. He took the call.

"Is that you, dear?" came his wife's voice.

"Yes."

"It's you, right?"

"Right."

"So you got your phone back."

K grunted in response. His mood brightened at the sound of her voice. It was definitely his wife, definitely her voice.

"That's good. So where are you now?"

"I don't think you know the area." In fact he didn't want to reveal where he was.

"Just wanted to remind you I'll probably be late—looks like we're getting together at Mom's place for dinner. Can you take care of your own dinner?"

"Sure."

"We won't be too late." There was an awkward silence. K was hoping his wife would say goodbye first.

"Sorry, dear—bye." She said it like a quiz show contestant mulling over possible answers.

K heard the click at the other end and closed his phone. His wife's voice comforted him, promised to extinguish the cascade of sentiments, each stronger than the previous one, that he had experienced that day: his feeling first thing in the morning that something was different, the unreality, the confusion, the sense of disorder amounting to chaos, the deceptiveness bordering on trickery, the soporific delusion you feel when you're running a high fever. And with the relief that followed came regret for his paranoia in jumping to conclusions about the woman in the video clip. "Sorry, dear," he mumbled to himself, repeating what his wife had said to him.

The woman in the video clip seemed familiar because she resembled his wife. But that didn't mean she *was* his wife.

But this brief interval of comfort soon lapsed into yet another bout of confusion. From the moment he had awakened that day he had encountered a variety of familiar individuals and presences: his alarm clock, his bed, their bedroom, his wife, his daughter, the puppy, his sister-in-law, his mother-in-law. And in contrast, a variety of unfamiliar counterparts: his own naked body, the matchbox, the gay bar, the wedding, his father-in-law, party B, the café woman's thigh, *City of the Blind*, seat C45, and the woman in the video clip. Yes, that was it—his anxiety rested on this helter-skelter mishmash of familiarity and strangeness, the juxtaposition of what he was used to and what he wasn't used to.

And wasn't it the same last night? He had drank with his familiar friend H. But could he be sure beyond a shadow of a doubt that it was H?

The clincher was his wife—her body in bed had felt like an anonymous corpse, refrigerated pending identification. It had lacked its familiar warmth. His wife last night was an unfamiliar other. Someone who under cover of darkness had slyly enacted the role of his wife. Although she was as familiar as his wife, she was not his wife, and that explained his erectile dysfunction.

So what happened to my real wife? And where's my real alarm clock, my real daughter, the real puppy? And what about my real mother-in-law and my real father-in-law? Did my father-in-law die, or is he still alive? Did party B actually find my phone in the theater? And who left it in C45? Me? A third party? And who left that video clip—me? Party B? Someone else?

And then the answer came to him—it was a conspiracy, a

mammoth conspiracy. What he had thought was reality was instead the huge setting of a play. His real wife had hired a stand-in. Like the spy in that old news clip. In preparation for his mission he'd lived in a re-creation of a city in the target country, familiarizing himself with life there, losing his accent, using the local currency and the public telephones, having sex with a prostitute playing the role of a local woman. He wore clothes the locals wore, purchased their commodities, got used to their daily life.

Had K been dumped on a set like that make-believe city? Was the woman he called his wife a professional actress, and his daughter too? If so, they were convincing in their roles—if not for the other strange happenings, K would never have suspected them.

But all the spy's preparations had been for naught—he had been captured. Just as there is no perfect crime, there is no perfect spy. Put a spy in an unexpected situation and he betrays himself. Maybe his radio communications are detected, or his accent slips out, or he draws attention by giving an extravagant tip, and a neighbor turns him in for a reward.

Then what about H? Well, he was a stand-in too, playing the role of K's friend. K was surrounded by hired stand-ins. He thought of surrogate mothers hired by childless couples and impregnated by the unfamiliar man. If the child is kept in the dark about the circumstances of his birth, he doesn't know about the surrogate mother in whose womb he gestated. The woman he calls Mommy is the woman who hired his real mother. He's the offspring of a monetary exchange and not the fruit of love. He has a mom and dad but in truth he's an orphan. And in truth K too was an orphan, an only child, an illegitimate child. A producer, more artful than the Great Creator, was looking down on K in his huge set, one moment chuckling and sneering at his unknowing subject and the next moment applauding him. His wife and daughter, the puppy, H, party B, his father-in-law—had they all been hired by the producer, had they all been trained in their role?

But there are always inconsistencies. Just as apparent truth can prove equivocal, inconsistencies based on the tiniest mistakes can eventually derail the grandest conspiracy.

A dozen or so people, more than for the previous screening,

had taken their seats. Skimming the new arrivals, K noticed the sexed-up couple in C37 and C38. Like him they must have arrived late, and they wanted to see what they had missed. But a closer look told him they were not the same. They wore similar clothing, gave off the same air, resembled the vacuous man and woman he had seen, but they were definitely not the same.

Then what about the others? The familiar faces were still there. Had they stayed behind to re-live the experience of communal laughter and weeping? Wrong again. They only looked familiar; actually they were new arrivals for the next show. The man in A27 had left and a new arrival was in that seat. Same seat, different person. C45 was where party B had sat, and when K left, someone else would occupy it. But the show time printed on the ticket gave him exclusive rights to it now—it would have been the same if C45 were a bench in a wooded park or a waterbed in a love hotel.

A matrix. The perforated block that stamps out masses of coins. A numeric grid. A mold for casting typefaces. A master for pressing vinyl records or transferring a tape recording. The indefatigable presses that turn out countless copies of counterfeit currency or reproductions of artworks. Gemstone ore. The meshwork of circuitry in a computer. All of these are matrixes.

Everything has a starting point, a motherland. What about humans? A womb is capable of producing identical twins, but not lesser reproductions, copies, fakes, or imitations. In other words, a mother's womb is not a machine. Then did the sight of such living, breathing human reproductions as he had seen today mean that K's own circuit boards were faulty?

K nodded. Yes, that had to be it. Familiarity was a deception. Familiarity and unfamiliarity were two sides of the same coin. The man now in A27 now resembled the man in A27 before, the young couple near K resembled the previous couple—in both cases, the individuals looked familiar but were not the same. They were like two sandwich men—the boards with their ads are familiar but the men wearing them are different.

Just as his familiar wife must be a stand-in, these moviegoers must be reproductions. Surrogate mothers are wombs that bear a reproduction of a human being. But a surrogate god can produce a mass-reproducing matrix.

Now that K had his phone back he had to see H. He found the number, entered it, heard the pop song H used for a ring tone.

"Hello."

"It's me." K kept his voice low.

"What's up? It's the weekend, don't you know?"

"I need to see you—where are you?"

A slight pause, and then, "I'm in my office."

"Your office. Don't *you* know it's the weekend?"

"I had something to do. But I'm almost finished—did you want to come over?"

"All right." K ended the call just as the chime announced the next showing of the movie.

Out of the blue K heard his mother's last words: "K, dear, come on now, get down from that ladder."

The last thing his mother had seen was a ladder of illusion, one you could not climb up or come down from. With that thought K went down the ladder from C45 and left the theater.

In front of the café where he had met party B, K encountered a woman. She looked familiar—it was that risqué woman, and she brushed his shoulder as she went by. It was as if she were waiting for him. K knew she'd done it on purpose, and when she said, "Oh, I'm sorry," he kept a noncommittal silence. What a stink, he told himself. She smelled like rotting meat.

Outside, the matrix woman turned back to ogle K. Was that a gesture? Her flirtatious gaze fused with the rays of the setting sun that reflected from the wall of glass windows. She disappeared around a corner. Blinded by the white rays, K groped his way toward the parking lot.

6:02 p.m.

Having parked in the garage below H's clinic, K found the elevator wasn't operating. Which made sense, it being the weekend. He would have to climb the stairs to the third floor. On the plus side, he wouldn't have to deal with that pain-in-the-ass of a nurse, thank

God. He managed to climb one floor too high, and had to reverse direction. The door to the third-floor hallway was open and the lights were on in H's clinic. Dusk was creeping along the streets below.

Sure enough, the nurse wasn't there. But someone else was, judging from the murmuring in the examination room. K found the button on the reception desk and pressed it.

"Is that you?" came H's voice over the speaker.

"Yeah, I just got here."

"I'll be out soon. Help yourself to the fridge."

The mini fridge was stocked with beverages. A can of beer caught K's eye. He settled on the couch, popped the tab, and took a drink. This was a psychiatric clinic—no disinfectants, no medical instruments—but it felt like a private bank for the wealthy.

K didn't trust psychiatrists. He knew that H took a conservative approach to medication for mental illness, though he did prescribe painkillers. K thought of H more as a spiritualist, a kind of psychic, than a doctor. It was a waste of time consulting with a doctor like H about anxiety and neuroses.

K knew that no diary was one hundred percent truthful. *Someday somebody's going to read it.* Anyone who kept a diary had this thought in the back of his mind—it was only natural. Likewise, none of H's patients would let down his defenses on the couch and spill out every last one of his secrets. The psychiatrist-patient relationship was a formality, the psychiatrist providing a high-interest loan for which the client mortgages his brain. Patient and doctor share secrets, H the accomplice and receiving a fee for his services. K had another swig of beer. Today he was visiting H not as a friend but for consultation. He was meeting with his accomplice. He would accept H's counseling about the turbulence, the confusion, the anxiety he had experienced all day. Unlike his previous visits, K felt as jittery as a cancer patient awaiting lab results.

Finally the door opened and H and another man filed out. The man was tall and robust—a wrestler, perhaps? K felt as if the man was looking right through him.

"All right, then." H held out a hand, which the man shook before retrieving a fedora from the coatrack and departing.

"Come on in," said H as he returned to the desk in his office. He buried his face in his hands. He looked exhausted.

K followed H and sank into the chaise lounge.

H got up and found a bottle of whiskey behind some books on a shelf. He filled his tea cup and promptly drained it.

"Care for some?"

K merely displayed his can of beer.

H buried his face in his hands again. His habit when he was in a fix.

"That crazy bitch." His voice was low but full of hatred. "Slut, shit-eating whore, mangy bitch in heat."

K knew all too well the "crazy bitch" was H's wife. But K had never seen H's "shit-eating whore" of a wife. The only times H referred to his wife with such vitriol was when he was drunk. But to launch in with such abuse after just a shot of whiskey, with no time for the alcohol to take effect, this was a first.

"I'm going to get back at her. She's so mean, that crazy bitch."

But if H's wife was the crazy bitch his curses made her out to be, then why couldn't he treat her? After all he was the expert in head cases and weird behavior. Poor guy, he must loathe himself for hating and cursing his wife instead of treating her—he was like Sisyphus, pushing his boulder up hill time and again. Wasn't it actually H who was the head case?

"What happened?" said K,

H knocked back another whiskey before answering. "Take a look." He held out a manila envelope.

K pulled the chaise closer, opened the envelope, spread the contents on H's desk. A group of photographs.

"Take a good look."

Nothing particularly eye-catching about them. They were Polaroid snapshots, and most were out of focus. K wondered if they'd been taken by a stalker.

There was a sequence showing a scarf-clad woman emerging from a building with a man, seated with the man in a car, leaning across the console to give him a peck on the cheek as they drove off. In the car her scarf was off and you could see her face.

"Who's that?"

"The crazy bitch, that's who."

Finally, thought K, *we meet in a photo.* She looked awfully familiar.

"How come you're so worked up over these?"

H heaved a sigh of exasperation. "Can't you see? The building they're coming out of? Arm in arm? That whore—that prick."

K took a closer look. Yes, the woman was indeed cozying up to the man. And the building bore the sign Paradise Inn.

"Well, maybe they weren't coming out from there—maybe they were just passing by."

"Oh come on—don't try to humor me," said H, cracking his knuckles in anxiety. "It's the scene of the crime for God's sake—they were helping themselves to some afternoon delight."

"How can you prove it?"

"I've got a witness."

"Who?"

"The guy who was just here. He's an ex-cop turned private eye. Didn't come cheap. I paid him to get me a moncy shot."

"Meaning they'd have to be in bed and naked, right? All you've got now is the arm-in-arm part. And you see that café in the inn—maybe that's where they're coming from. Plus, all you see in the car is a peck on the cheek, like she's saying thanks for the ride—it's not like they're French kissing."

"You couldn't care less," H shot back in a frosty tone. If K had become the defense counsel for H's wife, H was the scathing prosecutor. "If it was *your* wife coming out of an inn draped around some guy, if it was *your* wife in a car with her lips plastered against his cheek, would *you* defend her like that?"

It dawned on K as he weathered the protest that scarfless, the woman was the spitting image of his own wife. He re-checked the photo that showed her kissing the man. It was his wife's face, there was no doubt in his mind. But what was his wife's face doing in the photos? Was K's wife also H's wife? Was she keeping two husbands? Was polyandry alive and well in the new millennium? *Was that my wife in that inn, mating like a mangy bitch in heat? Was that my wife in the car kissing that guy?*

"Who *is* that woman anyway," said K, pointing to the photo and looking H in the eye.

"Who do you think it is—it's that slut," said H the prosecutor.

"And who exactly is the slut?" quibbled K the defense attorney.

"My wife—who else."

"You're sure?"

"All right, you've had your fun, now let's be serious."

"I *am* serious."

Like a defense attorney presenting evidence to the judge, K produced his cell phone and called up "my photos." Selecting one of the photos taken under the cherry tree in back of the rectory, he showed it to H, indicating the face of his wife.

"Then who is that?"

H gave it the barest glance, as if he'd been presented with a damaging piece of evidence, then glared in irritation at K.

"It's obviously *your* wife."

Which H would be expected to know, given that K's wife had once been his patient. But K didn't back down. Indicating the woman in the snapshot, he said, "Then is 'the slut' the same as the woman you see here in my phone, or different?"

H burst into laughter. "The slut in the photo is *my* wife," he said, pointing to himself, and then, jabbing K in the chest, "and that one there is *your* wife. You think I wouldn't recognize my own patient?"

"But," K persisted, "then how come the one in the photo and the one in my phone look the same to me?"

"It's just not possible. Your good wife and my old lady couldn't possibly be the same. They're different people," said H the prosecutor, brandishing the evidence as he cross-examined the defendant. "This is definitely your phone, right?"

"Right. Definitely mine—it has my wife's photo." K was tempted to launch into the saga of the lost cell phone—how he'd managed to get it back from party B, who claimed he had found it in a movie theater of all places—but then gave up on the idea. He didn't want to go back into that maze. Instead he decided to broach the reason for his visit. "But now that you mention it…it's been one hell of a strange day."

"Strange? How so?"

"I feel like something's wrong with me, like I'm not right in the head."

"For example," said H, giving K a piercing look.

"For example, it's like my wife is not my wife. And my daughter's not my daughter. And even the stupid puppy—somehow it's different from yesterday. And I went to a wedding today—my sister-in-law got married—and all my in-laws seemed like fakes. And on the street I'd see someone and then run into the same person again and maybe even a third time, but wearing different clothes—like the person was an actor. I feel like I'm having delusions, serious delusions—don't you think so? Your wife and my wife look the same to me. I feel like I'm getting paranoid, like there's a woman who's playing a trick on me pretending she's three different women."

"How could it be?" said H, clearly intrigued. He had a sip of whiskey. No longer the inquisitive prosecutor but once again the attentive psychiatrist. "You mean to say your wife doesn't feel like your wife?"

K thought through his answer very carefully. "If she's really my wife, then why don't I feel any intimacy when I'm in bed with her? Last night she felt like a corpse. How's a man supposed to get excited with a corpse—I couldn't get it up, for God's sake."

"Well, one possibility is you're experiencing something called dissociation. So let me see—where do you think your real wife is?"

"She's hiding somewhere and peeking at me."

"And controlling the fake wife while she's at it."

"Right. And not just controlling her—she *hired* her."

"What makes you think that?"

"That's what I'd like to know. The funny thing is, if we talk on the phone, it doesn't feel like she's the fake wife—it feels like she's my real wife, only she's been kidnapped by the fake one and hidden away somewhere."

H had another sip of whiskey. His rage toward his renegade wife seemed long forgotten. His eyes sparkled like those of a cat that's discovered a mouse.

"Here, have some," H said, pouring K a drink. "It'll help you relax."

K accepted the whiskey and had a drink. It burned as it went down.

"Let's try something." H turned on his laptop, pressed some keys, and a screen mounted on the wall lit up. "I'll show you an image and you tell me what it is." A click of the mouse, and a face appeared on the screen.

"Who's that?"

"Marilyn Monroe."

"You sure?"

K nodded. "I'm sure."

"And who's *that*?"

"Charlie Chaplin."

"I'm going to speed things up now. Keep telling me what you see."

The images that followed were a random assortment of people, places, and things, appearing in rapid succession.

"Obama, Kennedy, banana, Kim Chi Mi, tiger, Eiffel Tower, Great Wall, Park Chung Hee, Kim Il-Sung, Jesus, King Sejong, a cross, saxophone..."

H paused the display. "You sure about all of them—Obama, Jesus, and the rest?"

"Sure I'm sure."

"Then who's this woman?" H asked, pointing to the Polaroid of the woman coming out of the inn.

"Your wife, but she looks just like mine."

"Then how about this one?" H indicated the woman in K's phone.

"My wife."

"You're sure?"

"I'm sure."

"You said that on the phone you feel the intimacy you feel with your real wife—but in person she feels like a fake."

"That's right."

"Want to give your wife a call?"

"Here? Now?"

"Yes, now. You can use the office phone—that way I can listen." Before K picked up the receiver H added, "Give it your best shot—try to cozy up to her. You know, 'I love you,' nice and sweet. You *have* told your wife you love her, right?"

"Actually, I never have."

"Then what about sex—how often?"

"Once a week."

"How come once a week?"

"I don't know, like Sunday comes once a week, you know?"

"And is there some kind of signal you use when the time is ripe?"

K gazed at H. *What are you, some kind of pervert, you get off hearing about other people's sex lives, you like telling dirty jokes?* But he saw no indications of that.

"I tell her something like this. 'Tonight's the night—it's party time.'"

"And how does she react?"

"Most of the time it works. There *are* exceptions."

"Such as?"

"Like when she has her period, you know?"

"What's the connection?"

"I don't care for it—don't like the blood. It's like she's been stabbed, you know?"

"Does she like having sex?"

"She's not the type to show it, but I think she likes it well enough. But I can't really tell—I'm not her, you know."

H grinned. "So, you're lightening up." He gave K a pat on the hand, like a coach boosting the spirits of a sprinter, a swimmer, a weightlifter with a pat on the back or a playful slap on the cheek. "All right, let's make that phone call. Remember—be affectionate. And don't forget to tell her it's party time tonight."

K made the call, listened to the ringing at the other end, heard the echo as H turned on the speakerphone.

"Hello."

"It's me."

"Where are you?"

"The clinic. Thought I'd have a drink with H and then dinner. How about you?"

"We're having dinner at Mother's. I'll see you at home."

"Everything all right?"

"Yes, why?"

"Just wondering, you know…" K saw H winking at him. He got the message and proceeded according to plan. "You won't be too late?"

"I'll be home by nine at the latest. The girl is beat. Why?"

"I'm thinking, tonight's the night, you know."

"What?" As if she hadn't heard correctly.

H grinned at K and gave him the okay sign with thumb and forefinger.

"You know, party time, time for you and me."

"Dear, you're hopeless." And then with a giggle, "As long as you rise to the occasion." And then with a click the phone went dead.

And now it was K who felt like a hostage being manipulated by a kidnapper. His feelings were hurt.

"Bravo!" said H. "Swell performance. A star is born." He applauded. "So let me ask you—who was that woman you just talked with?"

"My wife."

"Your real wife?"

"That's what it felt like."

"So how is it possible that your real wife feels fake when you're with her but real on the telephone? You find this duality troubling, don't you? Apart from your family you have no problem identifying people, places, and things—Marilyn Monroe, Yi Sun-shin, and all the rest. But those closest to you—your family—and a few special cases you happen across, they feel fake, and you wonder if it's all in your mind. Maybe I feel like a fake too?"

K had a good look at H. It was H all right—not just someone who looked familiar, but H himself. He shook his head. "No, you're my friend H all right."

"I wonder if you're exhibiting a very unusual type of delusion," said H. "The Indian brain specialist Ramachandran published a study some time ago on a patient with Capgras delusion. His symptoms were similar to yours—he thought his father and mother were fake and they were deceiving him. But his case was much more severe—he was extremely delusional in fact. This syndrome drew a lot of attention after Ramachandran's findings were published, but it's still very rare, and I think we can say the delusions are different from yours. One more thing—did anything happen last night, a fender bender maybe, or a bump on the head, something that might have left you with a concussion?"

Well, thought K, there was that one-and-a-half-hour gap in the filmstrip of his memory, but he couldn't recall anything that might have caused a concussion. He hadn't noticed any marks on his head, no evidence of bleeding, no signs of trauma, no headache.

"The reason I ask is that the Capgras patient's delusions presented themselves after he was in a car accident—one in three Capgras patients has some kind of trauma or brain damage." H paused long enough to crack his knuckles again. "But no, I don't make you for Capgras. I don't see any indications of trauma that might have given you a concussion. So I'm thinking you might be having a panic attack."

"A panic attack?"

"It's increasingly common. Think of it in terms of anxiety, a fit of anxiety. Let me ask you—did you have any trouble breathing today, any tremors, any fears that you were losing control, that you were going crazy?"

K thought for a moment and shook his head. "No, nothing like that."

"What about sharp chest pains, a choking sensation, sweating?"

K thought of the wedding.

"Well, I did break into a sweat today, but I was hot and tired and stuck in a stuffy place—otherwise no."

K felt like a defendant trying to camouflage the truth about himself. He wished he actually had experienced a panic attack.

"Any sensation of unreality, or being awake and yet feeling you're in a dream?"

"Yes, feeling unreal, wondering if I'm having delusions—I've felt that way all day," K answered, relieved that his symptoms were in accordance with H's assessment.

"Then maybe it's *not* a panic attack. But one thing is clear — you've suddenly developed a phobia. Still, I could prescribe something for your anxiety."

So much for K's hopes.

"No, I don't want any medication."

To K's surprise, H was agreeable.

"And I don't want to prescribe it, either. Because I think that what you're experiencing is temporary. I have to wonder if you're overworking yourself. I don't think it's a major concern — it could have been too much booze last night, or maybe it's a mild case of trauma. Whatever, I'll bet some simple cognitive behavioral therapy will do the trick. It will involve your family, and I can give you some guidelines."

"Like what?"

"Well," said H with a hearty laugh. "You start with your party tonight — you've already arranged it. You put yourself to the test — do you still feel a lack of intimacy, does she still feel like a fake wife, do you still experience erectile dysfunction? Think of yourself as part of an experiment, a kind of guinea pig. Next you get together with the family member you feel most comfortable with — you get some comfort from that person, you recover your sense of identity. Can you think of who that person might be?"

K pondered, and his father's face came to mind. He felt like gagging. "Let me think about that," he said, suppressing the surge in his throat.

"Sure, take your time, no rush. In the meantime, how about I order us some sushi — there's a restaurant nearby. Now that you've told your wife we'll be drinking tonight, we might as well have a bite to eat beforehand. We can save time and hassle by getting it delivered. You like sushi, right?"

K was feeling a bit hungry. He nodded

While H was calling in the order, K closed his eyes. His father's face had disappeared. He felt his father had never existed, that, like Jesus he, K, had been birthed from a virgin womb, like some mutant. But strangely, he now recalled a story his father had told him — he'd probably been pestering his father for a funny story from the old days. He now lay down on the chaise and drifted into a half-sleep that felt almost like a hallucination. He could hear his father's voice:

Long, long ago there lived a father and son. One day the son pestered his father to tell him a story. And so the father told him a story. Like this: "Long, long ago there lived a father and son. One day the son pestered his father to tell him a story. And so the father told him a story. Like this: 'Long long ago there lived a father and son...'"

His father's made-up story, like a record skipping and repeating, was his way of entertaining little K. But instead of finding the story funny, K thought his father was weird. In his memory his father had the body of a lion and the head of a man—he was a sphinx. And every day that weird monster mauled K's mother and every night it gobbled her up. A cannibal who devoured K's mother. His mother, in comparison, was very special. The moisture in his eyes that he'd felt in that unfamiliar theater at the thought of his mother, moisture on the verge of gathering into tears, stemmed from the affection, the kindness, the devotion—all the feelings he had felt for her. But in his mind these feelings did not add up to love.

To K, *love* was a fabrication, a term used in myth; it had no counterpart in real life. It was thanks to his mother, and not love, that K believed in Catholicism, and it was thanks to the worry doll, and not love, that he believed in God, the worry doll symbolizing everything that would soothe a worried child. And the Christian teaching that it was for love that Jesus had borne the cross upon which he was nailed? A well-told tale like that of the Little Mermaid, who kissed her lover and then hurled herself into the sea to become foam. And the miracle of Jesus' resurrection was a fiction along the lines of the story of Snow White dying from a poisoned apple and being brought back to life by the prince on the white horse.

But apart from the ingenuity of Jesus' love and resurrection, and no matter what form they took—myth or legend, children's story or fiction—the church in which K heard them was a gathering place, a community center he had to visit once a week, it was like going to school. For K, attending Mass at that church had originated with his mother.

But even if the story of the Little Mermaid and the story of Snow White and the Seven Dwarfs were merely ingenious fabrications for children, first and foremost they were fun. Likewise, to K the church he attended was as intriguing as an amusement park with roller skating, bungee jumping, and a haunted house, or an arcade for grown-ups where children can sneak in to shoot imaginary enemies and drive hot rods.

K had cried when his mother died. The recollection was still vivid of his older sister giving him her handkerchief and soothing him—*There, there, don't cry, Mommy's gone to Heaven, don't be sad.* The very next moment, a face surfaced from the depths of his memory, a face he had long forgotten—that very same sister. It hit him like a familiar face on a wanted poster long out of date. Granted, he had always thought of her as Sister, this person who had given him her handkerchief and soothed him, but why the hell wouldn't her name come up? Was it JS? Not exactly a crystal-clear memory. She was his only sibling. What was their age difference—five years? He couldn't exactly remember. It had been so long since they'd seen each other, he almost felt they were no longer related.

I can take her or leave her—that's how K had felt about his sister. But she had adored him. One thing he had to admit: she had the conventional good looks that grabbed people's attention. She'd been a movie starlet and appeared in soap operas, but always in a supporting role.

"So what's your decision?"

K started. H was prodding him.

"The one you love and trust the most."

K opened his eyes. "My mother."

"Is she still alive?"

"No, she passed away some time ago."

"Then who else?"

"Well, I've got an older sister. But I'm not in contact with her—I don't see her. I don't feel like we're brother and sister anymore."

"That might work. Why don't you look her up tomorrow.

Who knows, maybe your feelings for a blood relation you thought you lost will be the key to rediscovering your identity. And don't forget to have a look through your family photos. That's crucial to treatment. The main thing is, carry out this plan, and then if your symptoms persist, come back and see me."

K nodded. "Got it."

And that's when the phone rang.

H answered, and a voice came through the speaker phone.

"Hello, is that you?"

"Yeah."

"What happened. You're not answering your cell phone. I've got dinner waiting—what's going on?"

The nurse's familiar voice.

"I can't make it—something came up."

At the sight of H so flummoxed he'd forgotten to turn off the speaker phone, K retreated to the waiting room and slumped onto the couch. If H's wife was "a crazy bitch," then that would make H, from her standpoint, a crazy bastard. And if she was "a mangy bitch in heat," then H was a mangy cur in rut. If the private eye had caught her in an affair by photographing her leaving an inn, then she could hire a private eye to learn through phone records if H was having an affair with his nurse. So if she was "a bitch," that would make him a bastard, and if she was abnormal, clinically speaking, then so was H.

Here's a guy who treats mental illness, and look at him—he's the fruitcake. Depraved son of a bitch, he's turned into a sex fiend.

8:53 p.m.

They were at the bar they had visited last night, outside Hongik University. Not a live music club for college kids, but a members-only establishment, farther from the hot spots, its clientele middle-aged men.

K and H, same as last night, had themselves a curtained booth. H called for his bottle, and it was delivered, along with ice and glasses, by a woman K took to be the manager. H gauged the contents and suggested to K that they finish what was left and call it a night. He poured himself a glass and drained it, all the while muttering "Crazy bitch" and "Filthy slut." It sounded to K like he had something caught in his throat.

Over in the corner a group of men were playing darts; an occasional cheer erupted from them. Out on the small dance floor a man played a saxophone.

"I've been meaning to ask," said H, "where did you run off to last night?"

"Me—I ran off?" asked K.

"Come on, don't play innocent. One moment you're here, the next moment I come back from dancing and you're gone. I figured you'd be right back, but an hour later you still hadn't shown up. Snuck off somewhere, didn't you?"

"What time was it, do you remember?"

"Maybe nine-thirty or so?"

K sipped his drink. That meant the hour and a half before he returned home at 11 was the dead zone in his memory. Once more he tried to recall where he had gone and what he had done in those ninety minutes. Was he abducted by an alien that implanted an amnesia chip in his head? Had he been mugged, hit over the head, knocked out cold down a dark alley somewhere? But then why only the cell phone—why would someone jump him just for that? And he'd already checked his head—no blood, no outward sign of trauma. Did that mean he'd been in another dimension, a place that transcended time and space? Had he died and come back to life? Even supposing he tried to explain this dead zone in his memory, he couldn't expect much empathy from H, so why mention it? Instead he concentrated on his drink.

"There was this book I read," said H.

There they were, the two of them, H and K, but instead of a dialogue, K felt like H was on stage performing a monologue.

"It was kind of funny. A man called John comes home from a trip and what do you know, his wife Mary is in bed with another guy. John flies into a rage. What's he going to do? He spots the other man's umbrella and destroys it. Then he says, 'You bastard, I hope you get drenched on your way home.' I feel like John. The best I can do for revenge is break an umbrella—it's pathetic."

He downed another glass of whiskey.

"You know the story of Ch'ŏyong, right? He comes home one moonlit night, sees another man sleeping with his wife, and sings a song: 'Coming home from a fun-filled night, I find four legs. Two are mine, but whose are the other two? Once mine, now taken— what am I to do?' But he doesn't get mad, instead he dances beneath the moonlight. And here I am dancing like Ch'ŏyong, the best I can do for revenge—it's pathetic."

K didn't get it—was H really that angry because of his wife's affair? It wasn't like H owned her. She wasn't an asset—a fancy jewel or a piece of real estate. She wasn't livestock, a nomad's camel or sheep. H's two-legged wife had entered into a marriage compact with him and they lived together, but did that make her his property? You could always break a compact, pay a fine, enter into a new compact. So why was H so angry?

If my two-legged wife and a two-legged guy—let's call him W— made four legs, I wouldn't get angry. It's a shadow play, that's all. But what I can't understand, what I can't fathom, is this—my wife isn't being an infidel, instead she's mocking me, deceiving me, she's a fake wife who's hiding her identity and playing the role of my real wife. An affair is like a shadow play of bodies, but lying is a dark shadow that sickens the soul.

More than anything else K loathed lying. He was proud to say that as far as he could remember, not once had he told a lie. What had thrown him into confusion all that day was not that his wife was being unfaithful or immoral, but his illusion that a fake wife had commandeered her and was operating her by remote control.

"I," announced H, rising unsteadily to his feet, "am going to dance. My only revenge. Like Ch'ŏyong dancing in the moonlight."

And like last night, H and a spider woman, arms wrapped around each other, began to dance. What a sight, thought K, H clinging to the tall woman like a droning cicada flush against the trunk of a tall tree.

He heard a ring from across the table—H's cell phone. K let

it ring a second time, then answered. It wasn't his phone, so he waited for the other party to speak first.

"Why aren't you picking up... hello... hello... now that you answered, say something... crazy bastard... dirty bastard... worse than a mad dog... I know what you're up to—"

K closed the phone. It must have been H's wife. He thought about the couple as he watched H clinging to the woman on the dance floor. Man and wife were playing hide-and-seek. Hidden in a cocoon of depravity, taking turns playing "it," taking turns peeking out.

Again the phone rang. K didn't want to deal with it and got up instead. Down the cramped hall to the men's room he went. Inside he found a man, arms propped on the washbasin, shooting up with something. He reminded K of a nurse giving a patient an injection in the buttocks, only the man was injecting his arm. The man was neither startled nor flustered. Nor was K, who proceeded to a urinal. Finishing his business, K went to the sink to wash his hands, whereupon the man removed the needle, tossed it in the toilet and flushed. There was a sucking sound as the toilet bowl drained. Once the needle had disappeared the man turned to K.

"God bless you."

K turned on the tap, noticed several drops of blood in the sink, washed them down the drain.

God bless you. God bless you. Meaning that the god of that man could bless him with whatever was in the needle? Meaning he could bless him with happiness and salvation?

K returned to the booth. No sight of H. He scanned the dance floor. Not there either. Nor was H's cell phone on the table.

K poured himself a whiskey and drank, then pressed the buzzer on the table.

The curtain drew apart and there was the spider woman.

"You called, sir?"

"Do you happen to know where my friend went?"

"No, but perhaps he went outside to take a call? It *is* kind of noisy here."

"Well." K checked his watch—10:03. "Would you please call a driver for me?"

Whether H had disappeared or merely stepped outside for a moment, K would shortly leave for home as planned. And because he was feeling the whiskey, a designated driver made sense.

"All right. In the meantime, would you care to dance?"

With a smile she extended her hand.

K wasn't inclined, but then remembered he had turned down a similar offer last night. And so he took the woman's hand and followed her to the dance floor. She signaled the saxophone player with a clap of her hands. The musician began a slow, languid tune and the lights over the dance floor went dim.

The woman fastened her hands around the small of K's back. She was about the same height as he, so there they were lips to lips, chest to breast, and groin to groin. K's chest was flat, hers was bulging; his privates were in relief, hers intaglio. And crotch plus crotch equaled four legs.

As she guided him over the floor, his head came to rest against her neck. Was that an insect? No, it was a tattoo. A tattoo of a butterfly, and so real K had the illusion it was alive. Wanting to chase it away, he gently pecked at the woman's neck with his lips. The butterfly remained. From it came a familiar odor. A revolting smell, of something rotting. The stink of decomposing garbage that even if bagged in several layers of plastic to keep it safe from stray cats, the smell finds a way out. *That woman!* The one he'd brushed past outside the café. And the stink she trailed—the peculiar mix of her foul odor and her chemical scent.

"This afternoon," K said to the woman as they danced, "you weren't by any chance at a café in Chamshil, were you?"

"I could have been," said the woman.

"And did you by any chance meet a man?"

"Possibly—I often do meet men."

K sneaked a look at her. She had the same hairstyle and the same black dress as the woman in the café, gave off the same stink, a stench he'd never noticed in other women. Add it all up and bingo, you had the woman from the café.

"You don't remember seeing me somewhere?"

"Well, I must have seen you here last night."

Her pinched voice and dreamy eyes made K wonder if she was high on drugs. Her tongue was pierced with a tiny bell that tinkled every time she spoke.

"Not last night, this afternoon."

"Yesterday, today, it's all the same. Anyway, I'm a butterfly." *Tinkle.* "I can fly anywhere—I have wings." *Tinkle.*

She's trying to deceive me. She wants to spy on me, she's been following me all this time, and now she's trying to tempt me.

The music came to an end and they ground to a halt. The woman wanted another dance but K declined and returned to the booth. Still no H. Enough left in the bottle for one more drink. He poured it and decided that once it was gone he would call it a night, regardless of H. While he sipped, the manager opened the curtain to inform him his driver was waiting. K handed over his car keys; he would be out in five minutes, he said.

He had a smoke. Feeling he had to leave unnoticed by the woman with the butterfly tattoo, he left the curtain open so he could peek out. There she was at the bar, sipping a drink and chatting with the bartender.

He couldn't understand why the woman was tailing him. He was just an average guy, and here he was being shadowed and kept watch over. He wasn't a person of grand ambition, had no secrets to hide, no ulterior motives, and he wasn't a criminal. He wasn't a drug runner or a smuggler, or an enforcer for a crime ring, or a spy, or a terrorist—no way. But today, if memory served him correctly, in a short span of time he had crossed paths with her three times. Was it mere coincidence? No, the encounters were deliberate, persistent even. Perhaps that woman had marked him at the wedding; maybe she would show up beside him in the family photographs. Finally, as she herself had said, they had met here last night. Who knows what might have transpired between them during the hour and a half he was in the dead zone?

K was peeved. He wasn't a dangerous guy. He wasn't paranoid about his wife's faithfulness, had never earned the distrust of his coworkers. He excelled at his job in the banking industry, was so meticulous in the execution of his duties he would never keep secrets or tell lies, and so he never triggered the suspicion of others. K finished his whiskey. So why would the woman with the butterfly tattoo want to harbor such strong suspicions about him?

Finally he rose. He was relieved to see the woman dancing with someone else. The man's hand had crept inside her skirt like a slug and was feeling around inside. After checking with the manager to make sure the bill had been paid, K went out to find his car idling in front of the bar. He climbed in the back seat and gave directions to the driver. As the car went down the alley he kept looking back,, fixated on the possibility the woman was after him. Not until they had turned onto the main street and entered the traffic flow, the familiar night scenes once again in sight, did K ease back in his seat. The warm interior made him feel tipsier. He nodded off, but just as quickly was awakened by thirst. And there was something about the driver. He was wearing a cap—a red cap—and it looked familiar.

"Would you happen to have some water," K asked the man.

"It just so happens I do. And I haven't cracked it open yet."

The man's eyes met K's in the rearview mirror. And then his right hand came off the steering wheel and in a gymnastic maneuver circled up and over the seat toward K—in it was a bottle of water.

"Thank you," said K as he uncapped the bottle and drank. "I'm thirsty."

"You're welcome," the man said, removing his cap for good measure to reveal his bald head.

Back on went the cap, but not before K noticed the bald head was familiar. Put together the familiar cap and the familiar bald head and he had a montage of a familiar face with cross-eyes—party B's face. The man who had saved K's cell phone, the insurance planner.

"What kind of work do you do during the day?" K asked.

Again the man's eyes were reflected in the rearview mirror. There in plain sight, cross-eyes—just as K had suspected.

"Mainly lounge around. If there was work... I used to do day labor—construction work—but those jobs are long gone."

"Didn't I run into you earlier today?"

"Well," the man vacillated.

So. Just like that, the job of tailing him had been transferred from the woman with the butterfly tattoo to party B, the insurance peddler. Like obscure actors taking on multiple minor roles to save on production costs, like extras might take on the roles of dead man A and passerby B, two minor actors, concealing their identities, were shadowing K in the guise of insurance man and designated driver, and café patron and private dancer. But *why?*

K was not afraid, did not know the feeling of fear. He wasn't a person who felt sad enough to shed tears, or happy enough to laugh out loud. Lying, harboring suspicion, jealousy, anger, sympathy for others, compassion—such feelings were irrelevant to him. He was a colorless man, one who lacked the palette of human emotions.

K went by the book. With him it was either yes or no, either black or white. Anything else was an untruth. If you had to pick a single word to describe him, it was upright. Never had he disliked another, suspected another, hated another, had an urge to inflict violence on another. And so what he felt from the surveillance, pursuit, and shadowing by the woman with the butterfly tattoo and the designated driver was not terror, was nothing akin to unease or fear. Rather, he felt disharmony, or perhaps a peculiar harmony, from a person previously familiar who now felt unfamiliar and different, he felt disorder from order, chaos in the universe, and antinomy in duality—in other words, he felt confused.

Before he knew it they were parked at his apartment complex. K added a 5000-*wŏn* tip to the fee.

The man doffed his red cap, revealing his bald head, and said to K, a twinkle in his right eye, "Here's my card—give me a call if you ever need me."

K pocketed the card. "Have yourself a good night."

The man donned his cap and left. K watched him cut across the parking lot and disappear. Finally—he was rid of his tail. Inside he went.

He entered the elevator and as he pushed the button for his floor, he recalled H's advice about tonight's party. As H had said, this was the only treatment that would corroborate K's complaints.

10:54 p.m.

His wife was watching television. Hearing K enter, their daughter emerged from her room to greet him in her singsong tone. The puppy growled at him, this time without baring its teeth.

The living room was nice and warm, maybe a little too warm. K hiccupped. Another of his reactions to alcohol.

"Do you need water?"

Without the elaborate makeup she'd applied for the wedding, his wife looked as unfamiliar as a woman you might meet at a formal marriage interview.

"Don't bother—I'll get it myself." *Hiccup.* K poured himself a glass from the refrigerator and drank it down. "I'll wash up first." *Hiccup.* A reminder that tonight was party night.

"All right. I'll be right along," his wife answered as she scanned among the channels with the remote. Surfing a dozen channels every ten seconds—that was her habit. If she happened upon a program that caught her fancy she would linger, but never more than five minutes.

Just as the image of a singer was registering in K's mind, it changed to a jet fighter, and then to lingerie on a home-shopping channel. K poured a second glass of water and went into the bedroom and undressed. From the drawer he took a fresh set of underwear and placed the items on the bed. Then he placed his pajamas next to his pillow. Into the laundry basket went his sweaty clothes. In the bathroom K fetched the packet with the two blue tablets he'd hidden in the washstand drawer.

He recalled what H had said when giving him the medication: "You have to take it at least thirty minutes beforehand. They're good for erectile dysfunction but they also crank you up psychologically—make you feel like you're the man."

And it was just as H had said—just the knowledge that he possessed this wonder drug made K feel he would be charged in minutes.

As he brushed his teeth he checked his aftershave—still Y,

and not his very own V. His stomach felt sour and he gagged. A smattering of fluid came up and he spat it into the toilet. *That's better*. After finishing with his teeth he stepped into the glass-enclosed shower and turned on the water. Out of the shower head, which resembled a withered sunflower, came cold water that quickly turned hot. Adjusting the temperature, he allowed the water to wash over him. And as he always did in the shower he whistled an impromptu tune, nothing recognizable either by melody or by rhythm. And then he got to work soaping himself and lathering up with the washcloth, to the point that he looked like a puppy shedding its fur. And the moment he lathered his privates he was erect, shameless as an uninvited guest, stiff as a flagpole, his penis having forgotten that its normal state was flaccidity, that expansion came only on an as-needed basis. K was flustered. He emerged from the shower, still at attention, and proceeded with his party prep — towel off, Q-tip and dry each ear, a splash of aftershave, then relieve himself. And finally back out to the bedroom and on with the underwear and pajamas.

He dimmed the nightstand lamp and lay down, ready to party. He assumed that in most cases it was the woman who prepared first and then waited for the man, but he held fast to his own routine, having never displayed his naked body to his wife. She must already have freshened up — after all he'd called in the party reservation early. If H was right in saying this was the only kind of treatment they could test to tackle K's condition, then K would be the guinea pig. *I'm a lab animal.*

"Did your hiccups go away?" she said. She had brought a glass of honeyed water, K's hiccup remedy. "Here, drink it, then hold your breath."

K did as instructed.

His wife undressed, starting with her blouse and then her pants. And there she was, bra-clad upper and panty-clad lower. K, who had never seen her naked, was taken aback by the sight of her with only her strategic parts covered. K located the lamp switch and turned off the light.

"How am I supposed to undress in the dark — I can't see a blessed thing," came his wife's voice.

K didn't see the connection. Even in pitch darkness people were able to undress. If a blind person could undress, then why not a sighted person in the dark?

Again K found the light switch; he turned on the lamp. One turn made it come on too bright, so he gave it a second turn. This produced a pale glow, not enough light to clearly distinguish objects but sufficient to help in undressing.

In full sight of K, his wife undid her bra. It loosened, exposing her nipples, which were the dark color of ripened fruit. Far from showing bashfulness she projected the stately presence of a lingerie model on a home-shopping channel. She bent to remove her panties. To K she looked like a stripper.

Once more K reached out for the lamp, and then all was dark. And with the curtains drawn, it was not just dark but wartime-blackout dark.

"What are you doing?" his wife called out. "Why are you doing that?"

"Don't we always party in the dark?" said K. He managed to refrain from adding that he'd never once seen his wife in the nude.

"Since when?" said his wife. "It makes me claustrophobic, like I'm buried in a mine."

K turned the light back on. His wife peeled off her panties as nonchalantly as if she was about to step on a pair of scales. There she stood, without a stitch of clothing. K was taken aback by the lush growth of hair at her crotch. She slid between the sheets and with a coy smile began to fondle him. Unmindful of the unfamiliarity of the situation, his penis remained at attention.

"Well," said his wife, excitement evident in her voice. And then her lips approached his face. "You're ready for action—not like last night." Their lips collided and her tongue slithered into his mouth, releasing a jet of saliva. And then it flickered around inside like the tongue of a snake. K felt pressured—it was almost like being raped.

No, thought K. This couldn't have been more different from all their parties until last night. It was sex for hire, for God's sake. It was unthinkable, his wife French-kissing him—that was something an escort girl would do. But one thing was the same as last night:

his wife was cold as dry ice. The affection, the intimacy, the sense of union between man and wife—he felt none of that from her.

No way could this woman be his wife. If the responsibility for tailing K had been passed from the woman with the butterfly tattoo to party B, the insurance man-cum-designated driver, then now the baton had been handed to this woman who was playing his wife. And if the café woman and the woman with the butterfly tattoo, as well as party B, the insurance man-cum-designated driver, were bit actors each playing two or three roles, then this woman playing his wife was the protagonist, a spy settled in her station.

Where had this woman been sent from? K was not a public servant or a high-ranking official with top-secret clearance. He was a deputy director in a bank. No spy would have tried to contact him for ideological purposes. So had this woman been dispatched from outer space? He could only wonder if an alien had arrived in a UFO to kidnap his real wife and then clone and replace her.

"What happened?"

Before K knew it his penis had shriveled. It looked like a strand of a dirty mop. His wife, or rather the unfamiliar woman who called herself his wife, who had squatted over K to receive him, clucked like a teacher confronted with a tardy student. Only she wasn't reprimanding the student, but coaxing him to be on time.

"Sorry—guess I had too much to drink," K ventured.

"You must be awfully tired." The woman gave K's bottom a playful slap. "It's all right, dear," she said, like a head nurse who knows better than to hurt a patient's feelings. "You'll be fine after a good rest, so off to sleep you go, all right, dear?" And then she lay down beside him. "But remember, that was strike two. Three strikes and you're out."

K reached for the lamp and turned it off. His hiccups had long since stopped.

H had suggested this experiment to see if K could rid himself of his unreal feelings of confusion and get his identity back. But the result was that it was all the more obvious that K's wife was not his wife. She was familiar all right, but in no way was she his wife. She was a fake. She was like a knockoff—same fabric and pattern, same stitching, same label attached to it, but in the end a counterfeit, a fake. But then *where* had his real wife gone?

The familiar and yet unfamiliar woman was snoring gently beside him. K turned off the alarm to make sure the clock wouldn't malfunction, as it had that morning, then closed his eyes. He felt lonely.

"Dear," K whispered. "Who are you anyway?"

"What?" came the woman's sleepy voice. "Did you say something, dear?"

"No," said K. "No, it was nothing. Good night."

"Good night. Sweet dreams. See you in the morning," she said with a lilt to her voice. In no time she was snoring again.

K felt himself hurtling down a slide that opened into dreamland. And then he was sucked deep inside.

SUNDAY

7 a.m.

What the hell? K groped the fuzzy boundary between sleep and wakefulness for an answer—what had awakened him?

His alarm clock. The strident ring a desperate cry letting the world know of its existence. Again the strident ring.

Dammit! He fumbled at the nightstand, found the alarm clock, silenced it.

He wasn't fully awake. But he was conscious enough to splice back together the snapped filmstrip of his interrupted sleep, and he closed his eyes.

Hey! Alarm—time to get up. He forced his eyes open, checked the display on the clock. 7 a.m. sharp. 7 a.m. He groaned. Time to get up. Time to get his butt in gear—get up, get ready, get off to work. He sat up.

Wait. Something wasn't right. Wasn't it Sunday? Yesterday was definitely Saturday, so today was Sunday, the second day of the weekend—he didn't have to go to work. Sunday—a day of privilege, a day he slept in, had a leisurely breakfast, lazed around.

Sure, it's Sunday, right? he clucked, easing himself back into bed. He tried to grasp the elusive remnant of his sleep, felt it twitching like the severed tail of a lizard.

It's Sunday all right.

He thought back through yesterday's events—the alarm clock, breakfast, the hair salon, the wasted trip to Janus, the wedding. That was Saturday, so today had to be Sunday.

And last night's party, at H's suggestion, the second night in a row. As his wife had put it, he had taken strike two, looking and not swinging, a rookie hitter—one more strike and he was out. But how could baseball lingo flow so easily from her lips? His real wife didn't know the difference between a strike and a ball, much less the complexities of the game. She had to be a fake.

In spite of his languid state, the mystery of last night had left unmistakable clues. K arrived at a conclusion: his wife was a fake— she was not the wife he had lived with for fifteen years.

His eyes snapped open. There, the curtain with its familiar pattern, the morning sun shining through the folds like fresh blood from a cut. Another fine, clear autumn morning.

K examined his surroundings. The polka-dot curtain, the Renoir reproduction on the wall, the hollow in his wife's pillow, the strands of her hair, the rumpled bedding, the nightstand, beneath the lamp the framed photo of their wedding, the door to their bathroom, the wardrobe with the door half open and revealing his wife's dresses. The familiar bedroom was his, but the familiar wife was not. She was just as fake as that alarm. And that was a conviction, not just an assumption—he'd caught her in the commission of her crimes.

Hadn't he checked the alarm clock last night, to avoid a repeat of yesterday morning's malfunction? And yet it had rung out, 7 a.m., on the dot, the strident wail depriving K of his hard-earned privilege of sleeping in. The clock's behavior was no less coincidental than his wife's—both were playing a trick on him. A ruse playing out to a precise timetable, the result of meticulous calculation, the events as fixed as the movement of a heavenly body.

Whoa, now, not so fast. K rethought his slapdash conclusion that his wife was a clone or a replica—even though the evidence from last night's experiment suggested otherwise. *Once is not enough.* In addition to that maxim he recalled the priest saying at Mass: "My brothers and sisters, a single mistake does not amount to a sin. Sin starts from a second occurence, a repetition that becomes a pattern and then an addiction." Last night's single experiment didn't amount to guilt for his wife. The verdict would have to await the results of the second experiment.

For the time being K could forgive her. The second experiment would be conclusive—he would know then if his wife was a fake. It wouldn't be too late to convict her then. Meanwhile the matter of her fraudulent behavior would be left in abeyance. *Lucky for you, I'm giving you the benefit of the doubt.*

From the kitchen came the clatter of dishes and the smell of buttered toast—his wife was up and about, fixing breakfast.

He took a sniff and muttered, "I'll forgive you for now."

He felt the urge, sprang out of bed, headed for the bathroom.

Tapping his full bladder, he watched the yellow stream foam up in the toilet bowl, noticed the alcohol odor. He flushed the toilet and took a deep breath. The mirror—yesterday's image of that buck-naked man had jumped out at him like an intruder. What would he see today? He turned, and there he was in the mirror, like a dove released from a magician's cloth. Behold, he was wearing pajamas. Thank God.

But before he could unwind, there remained the bathroom ritual. V, his signature aftershave—somebody had switched it. One petty detail, but it gave away the elaborate production that Big Brother was staging. But the aftershave would have to wait. First things first. He squeezed a large dollop of toothpaste onto his toothbrush and started brushing. Then filled his cup with water and rinsed. Then looked at his face in the mirror. His beard grew so fast, his face took on a dark shadow by the end of the day if he didn't shave in the morning. With his shaving brush he applied a generous helping of lather. As the razor began slicing through the lather, he felt the thrill of placing his neck on a chopping block. His whistling filled the bathroom.

Oops—he had drawn blood. A frequent occurrence. He stuck a piece of tissue to his chin. There—a nice clean shave. He looked much more cheerful. With warm water he removed the remnants of lather. And now, back to the aftershave. He took the bottle, gave it a shake like a bartender mixing his favorite cocktail, then applied a palmful. The aftershave was strong stuff. It felt like a branding iron on the nicks and scrapes. Then came an electric buzz that left his face momentarily numb. And at the same time, a fragrance so strong he didn't need cologne.

Wait a minute... K shook his head. It still wasn't his V. And the smell... It was like the stink given off by the woman outside the café. It was similar to the odor of the woman with the butterfly tattoo, a combination of a chemical smell and the stench of a festering wound. He checked the label. Brand X. Now he was really confused. V was the brand he'd always used, and yesterday it was Y, and today it was X.

What was happening? And then it occurred to him.

The Third Man, the invisible hand controlling all of these

games, hadn't been supplied with correct information about K's aftershave. Big Brother had the big picture, such as K's DNA, but not the fine details, such as K's fancies. This keen intelligence had picked up on K's suspicions about brand Y, and today it was trying out brand X on him.

I think, therefore I am. I am, therefore I am not deceived.

K glared at the Third Man. His first act of defiance against this absolute existence. He gritted his teeth in the face of this eternal, transcendent being, wherever he might be hiding, wherever he might be present, who existed not in the past, not in the future, but in the here and now.

"Just you wait," K spat. "We'll see what turns up tomorrow instead of brand X."

Big Brother had assumed K's alarm clock came on seven days a week instead of five. But in these niggling details he was making a mistake. And he still hadn't computed that K detested the sight of his wife naked. K took satisfaction from this finding. He wanted to stick out his tongue at this absolute entity, who was losing their game of hide and seek.

It was of course his fake wife who had set the alarm for seven and switched his aftershave. She was a daughter born of man, but she was brainwashed, a robot wired to be subservient to the prescripts of this absolute being.

K stepped into the shower, turned on the water. A shower first thing in the morning and then before bed—that was his habit. He preferred the one in the morning. Adjusting the tap to get the temperature just right, he blew out his breath like a lap swimmer and began to lather. He started with his chest, then his shoulders, arriving at his crotch. Unlike last night, no erection.

Emerging from the shower, he dried his face with the familiar towel and saw in the mirror his familiar face, like a reproduction of a portrait.

Combing his hair came next, and here he was especially attentive. He noticed the familiar scattering of gray, no different from yesterday. At first he had plucked the offending hairs, but before long it became a losing battle. If he kept removing it he'd end up practically bald. So why bother? But today he had an urge to pluck a few strands. If not, then he'd have to contend with the exact same image of himself as yesterday. He figured that just like rearranging the furniture in a room, removing some white hair would produce a change of mood. With the aid of the magnifying mirror he carefully pinched the first hair with his fingers. And then two more. Each pluck left a tiny sting, as from an injection. Three hairs and he was done. Depositing them in the waste basket, he decided to tend to his nose hair while he was at it, and inserted the small battery-operated trimmer in each nostril. It tickled, and he sneezed three times in succession.

Light of heart and whistling, he went out to the living room. Dazzling autumn sunlight flooded through the picture window that looked down on the main street.

His wife was at the sink chopping spinach. For breakfast K typically had salad—lettuce, celery, tomatoes, spinach, broccoli, onions—with a banana thrown in for good measure.

"Good morning, honey."

She didn't hear him over the *tock tock tock*. Instead of repeating the greeting K poured a mug of coffee and sat down at the table to his newspaper. He took a sip and savored it. *Good old coffee.*

Between sips he picked up the newspaper.

5.6 Earthquake Rattles West Sea Coast, 2 a.m. The front-page story, complete with a photo of several collapsed buildings. If there was an earthquake on the West Sea coast, then it would have been felt in Seoul. But K had been fast asleep and didn't feel it. He wondered if it was the aftershocks that had caused the alarm to go off and the aftershave to be replaced, but the next moment realized how far-fetched this notion was and dismissed it.

Once more he addressed his wife, but this time it took an effort. Would his wife's familiar face, unlike the aftershave, remain unchanged?

"Did you sleep well, honey?"

His wife turned to him. "Oh, good morning. No, I didn't— the shaking scared me. And then I saw the news about the earthquake. But you were out cold, snoring away."

K merely sipped his coffee and read. There was something about her tone—it was cloying, very much unlike her. And she was standing so close to him, too close for comfort. Instinctively he recoiled.

"Be careful today—they say there might be some strong aftershocks. How's the coffee, dear?"

"Good," he shot back, wanting to cover up his apprehension. "Really good."

Here he was playing to perfection his lead role in this large-scale production, this mystery show. A star was born!

10:05 a.m.

K had a hell of a time finding Café Eon—following an alley behind the new mega department store near Shinch'on Rotary, navigating a small open market, then turning down a street in a residential area. The department store was having a weekend sale, and the alley was a stew of uniform-clad whistle-tweeting attendants directing honking traffic into the parking garage, along with a throng of market-goers and packs of students from the nearby universities. It would take a man more intrepid than K to brave the chaos in his car, so he had parked some distance off and was making his way on foot to meet Professor P.

Shoppers, most of them women, jostled for position at the entrance to the department store.

K was undaunted by the prospect of reconnecting after ten years with the professor, his brother-in-law by virtue of having long ago been married to K's sister. Which was somewhat amazing considering he'd been out of touch with P for ten years.

Back then K had related better to P than to his own sister. For it was P who had introduced K to one of his students—and that student was now K's wife. As a young man K had little interest in the opposite sex, had felt no *zing* from women, had assumed he would spend the rest of his days celibate. Knowing this, P had encouraged him to give love a try and nudged him to marry, pinning him down with the argument that since he had deprived the young woman of her virginity he had to take responsibility. K had acquiesced. God only knew, if not for P, he might still be single.

P was a compassionate sort. He had felt for young K, who had lost both his parents, and was more attentive to him than to K's sister, the forgettable movie and TV starlet. K couldn't remember P's age, only that the professor was some ten years older and was something of a big deal for having picked up an M.A. in literature from a big-name university in the U.S.

And one day they had divorced. K never did learn why, though he had a hunch his sister had been playing around. Not once had K and P met after that, and K's contact with his sister had dwindled until they no longer communicated. He still had an occasional glimpse of her in a cameo role on TV, but then she vanished from the TV and silver screens as well.

Today for the first time in ten years K had tried to reach her by phone—the second of the experiments recommended by H for reestablishing K's sense of identity. He would test his kinship with her and revisit her old photos of their parents.

He felt awkward as he placed the call, as shameless as a moneylender trying to recover a ten-year-old debt—it was outlandish. After two rings there was a voice: *The number you called has been disconnected; please check the number and try again.*

Flustered, K had thought of P. P would know how to contact his sister. K knew they had a child and presumed P would be making child-support payments. P would have seen his boy from time to time (or was it a girl?) to stamp their blood relationship. P's phone number, like K's sister's, may have changed, but he should be able to find out from P's school where to reach him.

But first he tried P's old number and, surprisingly, it worked, even though the prefix had changed. Good thing P's name had come to mind.

"Hello."

Yes, it was P's voice all right.

"This is K, your brother-in-law. How are you doing?"

Brother-in-law—the first thing that had popped into his mind.

"Well hello—did something happen?" The tone was dry, but there was tension to his voice.

"I'm sorry to bother you, but I'm trying to reach my sister.

I don't have her current number, and I don't know where she is. I thought you might... Um, how should I address you now?"

"You can just use my name—that's what it's for."

"How about 'Professor' instead?"

"That's fine. But I'll use 'Brother-in-Law' for you. So how's your wife?"

Well, well, so Brother-in-Law, I mean Professor P, remembers she was his student.

"She's well. As I mentioned, I thought you might know of my sister's whereabouts."

"Indeed I do. As of three years ago, anyway. That's when she remarried. And when I didn't have to make support payments anymore. Not sure what's become of her since—whether she moved, changed her phone number, is still married, if she's still alive." There was a pause. "Sorry, I guess that's carrying it a little too far—but anything can happen in three years, you know?"

Sounds like he's starved for conversation, thought K. He sensed that P had relaxed his guard.

"But it's been so long, why don't we meet—we can talk more and I'll dig up your sister's number." And with that, P named a place K had never heard of—Café Eon, where he was now headed.

He had to hurry, it was almost ten, the time they had agreed to meet. Just as K spotted the café, a call from P arrived. Something had come up and he would be half an hour late—would K mind ordering first and waiting?

"No problem," said K. "Take your time."

There was a pause before P answered. "If they give you a hard time, or don't want to let you in, just tell them you're meeting Olenka."

"Is that a code? Do you have to be a member or something?"

"It's what they call me there—so try to remember it."

"All right."

Sunday morning, no other pressing business, and now he didn't have to rush—that was fine with K.

The café was located at the boundary of a residential area and the commercial area. The unpretentious sign made K think of a secret meeting place; it certainly wasn't intended to lure customers. K went down a stairway and saw on one of the walls a mural of the very same Renoir painting that adorned K's bedroom.

The café was not too big, not too small. In the dark interior he made out half a dozen customers, all of them women.

"May I help you?" a bearded man in a necktie asked cautiously.

"Could I get a coffee?" ventured K.

The man shook his head. "Sorry, we're not serving coffee."

He's lying. The place was fragrant with the aroma, and each of the women had a coffee cup at hand.

"That's strange, it sure smells like coffee — and isn't that what those ladies are drinking?"

"Ah." The man nodded. "We serve coffee to the public only on weekdays — today it's members only. If you're not a member, well, I'm sorry. Sunday we're open only in the morning and that's for our members. Please come back some other day. I'm sorry."

In contrast with the man's jagged features, his words and manner seemed artificially cordial.

K then recalled what P had told him. "Actually I'm here to meet someone. I think he might be a member — his name is Olenka."

"Olenka — Olenka, you say?"

"That's right."

"Oh, you should have told me. This way, sir." And after giving K a once-over, he led him to a table in the corner. As K was settling in, the man asked, "Would you like to use the fitting room or the powder room?"

K looked up at the man. A fitting room? That's where you change your clothes. And a powder room? That's where you fix your makeup. But this was a café, not a locker room at a swimming pool or a makeup room at a theater.

"No thank you."

"Well, if you change your mind, just let me know and I'll give you the key."

K caught the trace of a sneer on the man's face.

"Could I have some coffee, please?"

And voilà—a sign on the wall told him he was in a smoking area. He found his cigarettes and lit up.

Once his eyes had adjusted to the dim light, K found his gaze drawn to the cluster of women, who were sitting toward toward the far wall. Each and every one wore eye-catching clothing—almost like costumes for a masked ball. They looked like the women in the Renoir mural—long dresses, white opera gloves, white rimmed hats, parasols even. The images jumped out at you, like figures in a painting. K couldn't fend off the intuition that something was un-natural about them.

The coffee arrived. It was absolutely delicious.

K heard a bell ring. The door to the café opened and two men came in, all spiffed up. They must have been members, judging from the bearded waiter's warm welcome. They took seats not far from K.

Their coffee arrived and as they sampled it they all together shot K a look. Unfazed, K continued to savor his coffee. And then one of the men summoned the waiter and whispered in his ear, gesturing subtly toward K. Was he asking who K, the outsider, was? The waiter said something, whereupon the man nodded and vacated his seat. K noticed he was holding something. The other man cast the women an affectionate glance, then went up to them and began chattering away. The women responded with a chorus of laughter, and the man returned to his place. He still seemed to be suspicious of K.

K checked his watch. It was past 10:30, but still no sign of P. He held up his cup and signaled the waiter.

"Could I have a refill."

"Sure can." And the waiter obliged.

In between sips K crushed out his cigarette. He heard one familiar pop song after another—"Black Orpheus," "Barco Negro," and such.

From where the first man had exited, a woman appeared, like in a play. The woman sat next to the second man and helped herself to his cigarette.

K wondered where the first man had gone. If not for the musical sound barrier, he probably could have eavesdropped on their conversation.

And now the second man got up. He too slipped into what K now recognized as a back room. K lit a second cigarette—how else to kill time here. And the coffee had lost its taste. He kept his eye on the door, wondering when P would arrive.

A woman appeared from the back room and sat down next to the other woman. K felt like he was watching a magic show. The two men had gone up in smoke and the café clientele was once again all-female—with the exception of K, who felt very much the odd man out.

The door to the café opened, and there was P. K rose to greet him.

"Sorry to keep you waiting," P said with a searching look at K. "My wife grabbed me just as I was heading out."

K wondered if it was his sister P was talking about, then decided P must have remarried. But was that possible—he looked so old. Granted it had been ten years, but in those ten years P had become an old man. Not so much the white hair, but the way he had shriveled up and was stooped over.

P repeated his apologies.

"Don't mention it," said K.

The waiter approached. "Your key, sir?"

"You know the number?"

"I believe so—number 12, sir?"

"That's it."

And presently the waiter returned with a key bearing the number 12.

"And a coffee."

"Certainly, Olenka."

"You're looking good," P said to K. "Tell me about your children."

"There's just the girl."

"It's been that long?" P murmured. "My, how the time flies."

K noticed metallic objects on P's earlobes. *Earrings? How odd. A professor close to sixty wearing earrings.*

"About ten years, isn't it?" P continued.

"I think so," said K.

"Time passes so quickly. And all the changes."

"Not for me," said K. "No changes in the last ten years and I don't expect any in the next ten years." It came out sounding philosophical, though he hadn't intended it that way.

Being a humanities professor, P proceeded to indulge K in bullshit philosophizing, lapsing into silence only with the arrival of his coffee. He must have had something important to say but was waiting for the right moment to bring it up.

Finally P broke his silence. "I'll give you a heads-up—I'm about to change into a different person. It may come as a surprise, but try to understand."

"That's fine with me," said K. And since P was a literature professor, K thought of a literary metaphor. "As long as you don't transform into Kafka's centipede."

"I just might surprise you more than a centipede. Anyway, if you don't mind waiting, I'm off to the powder room." And with key in hand, he disappeared behind the counter.

K was puzzled. To his way of thinking, transformation was not simply a matter of changing one's outward appearance or one's clothing, but involved a fundamental change in shape, a metamorphosis, like that of a caterpillar into a moth. For creatures born from eggs it also meant metamorphosis in terms of the stages of growth to maturity. So what was P going to do—turn into Dracula and feast on human blood? Would he fly into a rage and turn green and muscle-bound like Hulk?

K forced himself to sip his tepid coffee while he waited.

After a time the door to the secret room opened and out came a woman who made her way toward K's table. She looked very familiar. And like the other women in the café she was dressed like a woman in a Renoir painting.

"Sorry to keep you waiting," said the woman with a smile.

K was at a loss. Here was a woman he'd never met, greeting him with affection.

"Hello—it's me," the woman said, gesturing to herself. Or more specifically, gesturing to her voluminous bosom.

And that's when K realized it was P. *So that's what he meant by 'changing into a different person.'*

"Tell me — what kinds of things do you like?" said the woman, or rather K's former brother-in-law. "You know, hobbies, interests, leisure activities? Hiking, stamp collecting, golf?"

"Well." Nothing came readily to K's mind, but he couldn't very well answer "Nothing" and douse P's attempt at conversation.

"I go to church every week. Though I guess you couldn't really call that a hobby or an interest."

"Why not? You go to church every Sunday and I come here every Sunday to dress up as a woman — that's my pastime. 'Eonism' in medical terms. It comes from d'Éon, a diplomat in the court of Louis the Fifteenth. He was a social butterfly, loved to dress up as a beautiful woman."

Which told K why the café was named Eon.

"I knew you were waiting, so I'm just 'up' now, not 'full up.' 'Up' means you're in women's clothes, 'full up' means you're all made-up as well — a complete transformation. So I just did basic makeup. If you don't mind, I'll finish up here."

"By all means, professor."

From a chic handbag P produced a mirror and makeup kit. Propping up the mirror, he began to apply more makeup.

"From now on I'm not Professor P or your brother-in-law, I'm a woman by the name of Olenka. So why don't you call me Olenka."

"I understand, Ms. Olenka."

Nothing so strange or uncomfortable about that. In fact K felt as comfortable calling P whatever he wanted, as he felt being referred to by his baptismal name, variously Pedro or Peter, or hearing his wife's baptismal name, Elizabeth.

"And you can drop the 'Ms.' Just 'Olenka,' and put some feeling into it — what do you say?"

"Got it, Olenka."

P grinned from ear to hear, his face overflowing with the joy. Just as a poet sang, "Whenever I call you, you appear before me as a flower," whenever K referred to P as Olenka, he could feel P coming alive in splendor, blossoming with rapture. The sad thing was, P was too old for the gorgeous display he was projecting, and the lush hair on his arms stood out in contrast to the meticulous women's trappings. Even more incongruous, he kept his normal voice instead of adopting a falsetto. On the other hand, his wig was exceptionally becoming.

Olenka continued to peer into the mirror as she applied mascara and then a hot red lipstick. Her eyes took on a lustful gleam.

"It wasn't until my late forties that I discovered my feminine side. One day I was going down an alley and I spotted a pair of panties drying on a line. And I stole them. And tried them on. You wouldn't believe how happy I felt. As Aristophanes said in Plato's *Symposium*, 'In the beginning there was man and woman and a third gender that was both man and woman.' Man was sun, woman was earth, and man-woman was moon. Man-woman, this third human type, actually came first. But Zeus could not tolerate man-woman's growing pride, and he divided man-woman in two. The man and the woman that resulted were left to wander the earth, each in search of the other half. It was man-woman, this third human type, that was the origin of humanity, and in the future it would become known as *Homo ludens*, the most advanced species of human. If man-woman had flourished, we wouldn't have sex crimes, gender discrimination, gender inequality, you name it. The family would be a place of freedom, a site of gender liberation—don't you see? Now don't get me wrong. I myself am not bisexual, and I'm definitely not homosexual. It's just that somehow I'm stimulated by dressing up as a woman—but my transformation ends there. It's all about peace of mind, simple as that. I hate it when people approach us thinking we're gay. I believe a husband can play the role of a wife, and a woman can play the role of a man—why should they be limited to husband or woman? I think gender can be communalized—that the family can be a paradise on earth, a place where there is no such thing as possessiveness or jealousy."

"Does anyone know you turn into Olenka every Sunday?"

"Not a soul—not even my wife, and definitely not my son. Oh, I forgot to mention, I remarried five years ago—sorry, I guess you don't want to hear that."

"Please, never mind, Olenka."

"Olenka — it's a beautiful name, isn't it?"

"It's different, I'll say that — doesn't sound British or American."

"It's Russian. Olenka's the protagonist of the Chekhov story 'The Darling.' The name is lovable, just like the title."

"Do you wish you were a darling, Olenka?" K asked playfully.

K's eyes met Olenka's in the mirror, and K instantly noticed their sensuousness.

"If only. Oh yes, if only."

A man who wants to return to his mother's womb, thought K. And be reborn as a pretty, lovable lady.

"The reason I suggested we meet here is that Sunday is members-only and if I skip it I really suffer the rest of the week — it's like a panic attack, or a woman's monthly cycle. And I figured I could trust you to keep it a secret..."

With a few dabs of the powder puff Olenka finished her makeup. The mirror snapped shut and back into the handbag it went with the makeup kit.

Olenka's femininity was striking, but to K it was freakish. On the other hand, a drag queen in such an outfit wouldn't be considered out of place. People were getting better at not eyeballing others in public. And P could do just fine in the role of Olenka the pretty lady. A perceptive person could see through the disguise, but as a drag queen Olenka would experience gender liberation, as P had put it.

"Now, down to business. This is the number I had for your sister three years ago, and I'm guessing it hasn't changed." Olenka passed K a slip of paper, which he pocketed. "She's a good woman, your sister. She really loved you. She was always worrying about you — my little brother this, my little brother that. Of course, I shared her opinion of you."

"Yes, Olenka, I know."

"Three years ago I heard she remarried. I truly hope she's happy."

"I do too, Olenka."

"There's another reason I wanted to see you — I want to buy

something for my son. You remember we had a son, right? I used to see him now and then, but not now that I have a new family."

"You had a boy?"

"Yes, a son. And it's been a while since I've given him any-thing. I thought you might be able to deliver a present for me."

"Of course, Olenka."

"There's a department store near the rotary. You probably saw they're having a sale. If it's all right, I'd like to go there with you."

"Of course, Olenka."

"If you don't want to be seen together, then I'll just follow you."

"Makes no difference to me. You look fine the way you are."

"All right, then, shall we go?"

They rose together, the waiter approached, Olenka spoke. "We're going shopping. I'll pay when I get back."

"All right, Ms. Olenka."

When they reached the door, the other women all rose.

"See you soon, Big Sister."

A gesture of respect toward an elder, thought K.

One of the men K had seen pre-metamorphosis gave an affec-tionate wave of her white-gloved hand.

"Good to see you, Jessica," responded Olenka with equal af-fection. "And you, Nan-jŏng."

Up the steps and out onto the street went Olenka. The au-tumn sun reflected from the alley as though it was lined with shat-tered glass. On went Olenka's sunglasses and up went her parasol. K had reservations about the parasol. It was too old-fashioned, the kind of knickknack you might find at a flea market. And instead of screening her from view, it drew people's gazes. Most of the pass-ersby gave her a glance, but Olenka seemed to enjoy the attention.

"Shall we?" said Olenka, offering a white-gloved arm to K. K linked arms with her and down the street they went, side by side. K thought initially she had made the suggestion so she could enjoy her transformation into a woman. But before long he struck upon another reason—perhaps Olenka's stiletto heels were too high and a supporting arm offered the safety that no amount of practice could offer. In any event, arm in arm the two of them looked like an affectionate couple.

A boy band was performing at the department store plaza to a throng of cheering, screaming girls. Olenka was taken with the scene, and K came to a stop alongside her as they watched the group sing and dance.

"When I'm full up I sometimes get a violent sexual urge," she said. "I want to relieve that urge, even if I have to masturbate, but I'm able to control it." She said it straightforwardly, with no insinuations K could detect, then folded her parasol and led K inside the store. She seemed to know the layout, and they took the escalator up to the third floor—women's apparel. Unmindful of the stares, Olenka scurried to the lingerie section.

"I just want to look around—Idont't plan on buying anything."

The sales clerks seemed to know her and they gathered about. K had a rest in the small sitting area, like a husband waiting for his wife to finish her shopping.

Various items of lingerie were on display. Bras, risqué thongs in blazing colors fit for wear by a prostitute, slips, drawers, halter tops. Olenka examined each and every style, a clerk always there to advise her. She was as blissful as a woman strolling in a park where the flowers are in full bloom. Finally she selected a pair of fishnet stockings and a sheer crotch thong fit for a porn star, and they were bagged for her. The thong was too tiny to have concealed her privates and looked feather-light, but had clearly quenched Olenka's thirst. *And that's all that counts*, thought K.

Their next stop was casual wear for teens. Olenka purchased a winter parka and a pair of pants.

"I'm pretty sure he's thirteen, but this is for a fifteen-year-old. He can always grow into them if they're too big, but they're useless if they're too small. So, you'll give these to him?" Olenka handed K a gift bag with the items wrapped inside.

"You can count on it, Olenka."

"And if you could tell him this—that his dad loves him. Or you can say I miss him. Use your own judgment."

She's lying, thought K. She didn't love the boy or miss him any more than the customer is king, in the words of a department store sales pitch. But he agreed to do as she asked.

Outside the store Olenka unfurled her parasol.

"We might as well say goodbye here—since I'm going back to Eon."

"Thank you for the coffee, Olenka."

"So long," said Olenka as she offered an opera-gloved hand. "I know I ought to take off the glove first, but I'm still Olenka. It's not a breach of etiquette, right, keeping your gloves on?"

And there they shook hands. Off went Olenka toward the café, back went K toward the parking lot. Along the way K looked back. He saw the bobbing head of a giant in spike heels, holding her own in the surging human tide, straight and tall as a poplar.

11:53 a.m.

Campus Boulevard, where the university used to be, was a hodge-podge of quirky shops, little theaters, subterranean clubs, and galleries. Garage bands were performing in the park that fronted the former administration building. Pigeons swooped about and ginkgo trees were in radiant splendor, resembling golden yellow gas lanterns.

The least he could do was bring a gift, thought K. It was after all ten years since he'd seen his sister. He spotted a familiar bakery—perfect. K purchased a birthday cake, along with bean-jam buns and cream buns; he explained they were a present, and the clerk gift-wrapped the items.

His next destination was a pharmacy. He still felt a dull pain, with occasional stabs, where the puppy had bit him yesterday, and he wondered if an infection had developed. It might be a good idea to wipe down the area and wrap it. And buy a pain reliever as well. But both the pharmacies that caught his eye were closed. Back to his car he went, and he set off up the hill behind the boulevard.

"Oh my god!" cried his sister when he had called her shortly before. Her voice was the same as he had remembered. For a moment K was too choked up to say anything. Whether from the emotion of their blood relationship or from the knowledge that just the two of them were left and she sounded overjoyed recognizing a voice she hadn't heard in ten years, he didn't know. When K had explained that he wanted to see her, she had responded that actually she had missed him all this time and felt apologetic about the last time they had met. K wasn't sure what she meant by "the last time" but felt she was sincere about wanting to see him.

She gave him directions to their apartment, then said that since it was lunchtime why not eat together—though she didn't have anything special prepared. It was almost as if she were expecting him, thought K. Almost as if the Third Man had informed her in advance of K's visit, and she was responding with appropriate gestures of delight, apology, and invitation.

As he began the steep drive up into the Naksan area he pondered the riddle of "the last time," mentioned by his sister. When was "the last time" and what was it all about? Did it have something to do with her divorce from P? Was she wishing she'd contacted K about her remarriage three years ago? Or was she simply apologizing for falling out of contact?

The apartment complex was public housing that consisted of a few five-story matchbox-shaped buildings perched on top of a hill. K had never realized that these swallow nests existed here, teetering on the summit, high above Campus Boulevard. The buildings were old and dilapidated. Held back by a retaining wall, they resembled a fortress.

K parked in front of building 3, as directed by his sister. The gaps between the buildings offered a sweeping view of the city center, which from this high vantage point appeared to be kneeling down in submission. K would have to climb to the fifth floor—complexes this old didn't have elevators.

Couples squabbling, children crying, the smell of bean-paste stew, the shouts of children on bicycles, clotheslines with laundry drying in the sun, random outcries, squawking televisions, the amplified voices of merchants hawking vegetables in front of the buildings, the distant roar of traffic, honking and all, sounding like the ocean; a boozy, raspy singing voice jousting with a harmonica, the yowling of stray cats chasing mice down the halls, the stink of garbage pails from those same hallways; body odor fanning out from every apartment whose door was open, the occupants not caring if they were in public view; the sharp chime of clocks striking twelve. All of these sights, sounds, and smells were captured in the specimen net of K's senses. All together a familiar spectacle.

His sister's unit was the last one to the right on the top floor. Attached to the closed door was a cross with the name of a church engraved in it. Did this mean his sister attended that church? Or was it simply an ornament? His sister used to be a more devout Catholic than him. Thanks to their mother. Her sister had married P in a Catholic church. K wondered if she had converted to Protestantism, given that divorce was forbidden by the Catholic Church. Perhaps she no longer set foot in a church, maybe she had turned into a cold-hearted atheist. Maybe the church on the door wasthe one her thirteen-year-old son, K's nephew, attended, or maybe it was where her new husband, K's new brother-in-law, went.

He pressed the doorbell.

"Coming!" And the next moment the door opened. Before K stood a large woman with a broad smile. She didn't look familiar. It took a few moments for him to recognize her. His once svelte and pretty actress sister had ballooned into a grossly obese woman who must have weighed a good 250 pounds.

"K, I can't believe it's you—come on in." Her voice was the same, as clear and high-pitched as a castrato's.

K entered, shopping bags in hand.

"I'm afraid it's not much to look at," said his sister as she guided him in.

It was a hot day and the windows were wide open. There was an unobstructed view of downtown. K felt like he was in a cottage on a seaside bluff looking down on the ocean at low tide. He could see that his sister had given the living room a quick sweep in anticipation of his visit, but it was still a mess aand probably always had been.

"Sit, sit. Let's have a look at you." And after she had seated him on the couch she took his face in her hands, which she had cupped like a volleyball player receiving a serve. "You're just the same. Some gray hair, a few wrinkles, otherwise the same. But how long have you had glasses?"

"Four, five years, I guess. My eyes started getting bad..." It was so long since he'd seen her, he wasn't sure how casual he should be in his speech.

"But I've changed a lot, right?" she said, giving his cheeks a playful pinch.

Indeed she had. Her former slinky build had filled out so she looked like a humongous boar, and her beautiful, soft, auburn hair had turned coarse and lusterless, and limp as frost-ruined *bok choy*. The plastic surgery on her eyelids and nose during her and probably always had been. had broken down, her eyes swollen as if diseased and her nose squashed like a melted candle that had rehardened. Her wrinkles made her look older than her age. And her hair had been dyed so long ago that only the outer layer was still black; beneath was ash-gray and the crown was white.

Her makeup must have been a rush job. The lipstick resembled ketchup smears, her eyebrows rough sketch marks. Her nonchalance was manifested in her loose, sacklike garments, in which her obese form jiggled like carelessly wrapped cuts of meat.

Her lovely figure had suited her well to glamour girl roles. But now her braless breasts were practically in full view, her obesity making her ample bosom even larger. She looked like a porn queen with breast implants.

"Look what time has done to me," she sighed, as if to emphasize that her disgraceful appearance was no fault of hers. And then, indicating the shopping bags, "What's that?"

"I called P to get your phone number and we met up this morning. He wanted to buy your son a present so he got a parka and a pair of pants at the department store."

"That clueless idiot." She ripped off the wrapping paper.

"And he made a point of asking me to pass on a message for him."

"Oh, I can't wait to hear this."

"He said he missed the boy. And something else."

"What?"

"He loves him. So, he misses him and he loves him—that's the message."

His sister framed the parka against her body, a giant trying on a pygmy's garment.

"Where is he, anyway?" asked K.

His sister fixed him with a look. The bedroom door was closed and from inside it there came a constant rattling sound.

"In there?" K gestured toward the room.

"He died three years ago. He was playing in the water and he drowned." She said it matter-of-factly. "The idiot should have known—I'm the one who told him. And now he wants to give his dead son something. He loves him. He wants to see him." And then, pointing to her head and making a circle, "A guy who doesn't remember his own son is dead is a crazy bastard, pure and simple." As she made the crazy motion, the line of her panties came into view through the thin fabric of her sack garment, their pattern as titillating as that of the panties that P, or rather Olenka, had bought at the department store. In spite of her 250-plus pounds of bulk, his sister's body could still turn heads.

"And that?"

"I bought a cake."

"Well, thank you—I've always liked baked goods, you know." So saying, she set the cake on the dining table and sliced it with the plastic knife. Loading a helping onto a plate, she began wolfing it down.

She's a compulsive eater, for God's sake.

"Want some?" she asked perfunctorily, not bothering to wipe her frosting-covered lips first, and in no time the serving of cake was gone. She dug into a second slice, not so much eating but popping it down her gullet. And then, wiping the frosting from her mouth and where it had dropped to her chest, then licking her fingers, she resumed talking.

"How's your wife? And your daughter? She must be pretty big by now. She was three years younger than our boy, right? Which would make her ten this year. I got an idea—you take these and give them to your daughter. There's no boys clothing or girls clothing now anyway—everything's unisex. They're probably too big, but better big than small—she can wear them later on."

It was a sham attempt at a conversation. She wasn't expecting a response from K, merely wanted to distract him from her disgusting gluttony.

"So who does she take after—your wife? And you must be getting ahead in the world, you look so neat and clean. Now that I think about it, you always were a neatnik."

In no time half the cake was gone. His sister turned to the buns with the look of a contestant in a pastry-eating contest.

Just then the rattling from the bedroom stopped, the door opened, and a man emerged. K's sister paused long enough to say, "Honey, there's someone I'd like to introduce you to."

The man wore gaudy hiking attire, and had a rucksack slung over his shoulders. Ready to head for the hills.

"I told you," his sister said to K, "I told you I remarried, right? This is my hubby."

The man removed his cap, considered K, then offered his hand. "She's told me about you. Pleased to meet you."

K regarded the man. He looked very familiar. No, it was more than that. *I know this guy.* It was the mysterious father-in-law from his sister-in-law's wedding yesterday. K looked more closely, wondering if his eyes were deceiving him. No, the man had the same blacker-than-black dyed hair, the dentures so white they looked bleached, the same hand that had gripped his, the same unusually wrinkled face. It was his father-in-law all right, the father-in-law K had thought was dead.

Didn't I meet you yesterday—

The question was on the tip of his tongue but K managed to suppress it. If his wife was to be believed, her parents were divorced at the time of her wedding with K fifteen years ago, and the divorce was covered up with the lie that her father had died in an accident. And so the man K had thought was dead had married his sister. K's father-in-law yesterday was his brother-in-law today.

"Have a good visit," said his father-in-law, or rather brother-in-law, as he donned his cap again. "I'm off to meet my hiking buddies." He smiled. "Don't be a stranger." And then he was gone.

K was baffled. His tailing by the exhibitionist woman at the café yesterday had continued into the night at the bar, ending with the designated driver who had given back K's cell phone earlier in the day. And then the job of surveillance had been handed over to his fake wife, the residential spy. And now the remote control had passed on seamlessly to his father-in-law, or rather his sister's new husband, or rather K's brother-in-law, so that K's every movement was being watched and recorded.

And if that was the case ... was this behemoth of a woman without a doubt K's biological sister? Or was it possible she was a fake?

He shook his head. No, she was his real sister. Time and weight gain had led to a drastic change in her appearance, but K felt the intimacy of a sibling relationship, the affection and thermos-hot warmth from his sister that had been lacking in his wife last night. *She* is *without a doubt my sister.*

It was a good thing he had sought her out after all these years. As H had suggested, she could play a pivotal role in K's attempt to recover his confused identity, could be decisive evidence in unmasking the labyrinthine conspiracy that had enveloped K.

And now he had to try out the next part of the experiment.

"You have a photo album, don't you?" he asked his sister.

"Album?"

"Yes, family photos from when we were young. With Mother and Father."

"Oh, *that* album—of course." She nodded. "And not just Mom and Dad—there are some of you and me too."

She began looking through the living room, the mounds of her flesh revealed in silhouette through the thin fabric of her clothing. Without a bra her breasts were jumped into view, the dark nipples projecting like a pair of thick, ripened grapes. And when she bent over in search of the album, her huge buttocks came into sight, as well as the dark pubic hair escaping her panties. She looked like a jaded housewife making a play for a traveling salesman.

K couldn't understand why, in spite of his best intentions, his gaze had followed the outlines of her body and come to rest at that particular place. He drew solace from the sense of closeness, the intimacy of their sibling relationship, but he had to be honest with himself—wasn't that gaze also an expression of his lust?

Finally she found the album, and drew up beside K on the couch. She smelled of perspiration. It wasn't a bad smell, actually rather comforting, redolent of love and affection. And the next moment came the perception—it was the smell of his family from back when he had been in their embrace.

"Let's have a look," said his sister. "These are just of our family. And you know what this is?" She indicated a four-leaf clover mounted on the first page. "I found it at Tŏksu Palace. I was in college then. The three of us were there—Mom and you and me. Remember?" Arm around K's neck, she pulled him close. "You little brat, where have you been all this time?" She smooched him all over and then came a peck on his lips. "I'm sorry about last time. But as you can see, I was hardly in a position to help anybody out. I'm really sorry, I hope you'll forgive me."

K still couldn't understand what she was talking about, and when she proceeded to stroke his ear, he shrank back even as he felt something quicken inside him.

"All right, you help herself and I'll make some lunch. You like noodles, right?"

She remembers what I like! Yes, she was his sister all right.

"In cold *kimchi* broth," she added before disappearing into the kitchen.

K hung his jacket and rolled up his pants legs to make himself comfortable, and looked through the photos. There were shots of his father, who had died when K was ten or so. He was wearing his military uniform. *Oh, that's right, he was in the military.* Without a doubt he was K's father, but K felt nothing from the photos. To K he didn't even rate as an adoptive father. K felt like he was virgin-born.

But with his mother it was different. He was snared in a tangle of emotions at the sight of her, and his eyes grew moist.

And then a photo from back when they were all there, his mother and his father and his cutie of a sister all dolled up—had they actually existed, or were they merely the random subjects of photos entered in a contest? They resembled characters in a scratchy print of a silent Charlie Chaplin film, all of them long since dead and gone. His family, were they anything more than stuffed figures collected in the specimen net of his memory, in the same way insects had been mounted in his specimen album?

Were they like mounted insects that once were alive, a fluttering butterfly, a dragonfly, a dung beetle? Were they like stuffed animals in a museum display, creatures that in life had bounded over the grasslands, a leopard, a deer, a giraffe? Had he really existed, the father who had told him the *Long long ago there lived a father and son, and the father told the son, "Long long ago there lived a father and son"* story, or was he a ghost? But unlike photos of other families, in this photo it was his mother alone who came alive, like an insect just added to the specimen bottle, still buzzing and flitting about.

K, his mother, and his sister, they were doubtless a family. The photo of K and his mother at his primary school graduation was clear evidence of that. K was wearing the standard student uniform of the day, the white collar standing out against his crew cut. He proudly clutched the tube containing his graduation certificate. His mother wore a *hanbok* and embraced him from behind; in her eyes he was the most precious being in the world.

K selected two photos to keep. The first was the primary school graduation photo with his mother. The second was taken at Tŏksu Palace and included his sister as well. She was in college then and then because she looked more mature. K was in middle school and starting to go through puberty. His sister had discovered the four-leaf clover that day and mounted it on the first page of the album for good luck. But her life was far from lucky. The photo was like a freeze-frame from a film. Those two photos could become a crucial part of K's treatment.

K recalled a therapy H had once mentioned—mirror therapy. It had become the standard treatment for those who have lost an arm but continue to feel severe pain in the missing limb. The patient realizes through looking in a mirror that the pain in his missing arm is not real but results instead from a delusion that all four limbs are intact. Likewise for K, these two photos would prove effective in helping him recover his identity. As long as his memories of Mom remained intact, there would never be a fake mom, and as

long as he could feel the existence of Sister, there would be no dupli-
cate sister. The undeniable existence of his mother and sister would
wake K from his nightmare and release him from his brainwashed,
hypnotic state.

The second half of the photo album was like a tour through
his sister's life. Many of the photos had been ravaged, his sister appearing to have taken the scissors to them. The missing parts must
have been her former husband and her son, the drowning victim. K
saw no reason to look further and closed the album.

While K was selecting the two photos his sister was in the
kitchen preparing lunch—boiling soba noodles and rinsing them,
garnishing the noodles with chopped *kimchi* and *kimchi* broth and
water, and adding a dollop of sesame oil and some ice cubes. All the
while she was singing in a loud voice:

> *Oh, oh, what should I do?*
> *Here we are, circling each other*
> *Time waning, our relationship fading,*
> *it scares me so.*
> *Oh, oh, what should I do?*
> *Here we are, circling each other…*

The same verse over and over, like a broken record.

K heard her washing her hands, and then she appeared.

"Here we go."

As they ate, K held up the two photos from the album and
asked if he could keep them.

"Of course. I used to look through the album when I was
feeling down. You take them—you can get some comfort from
Mom when *you* feel down. Do you remember how much she loved
you? You were her hope, till the day she died."

Sticking the two photos in his wallet, K thought back. He
and his sister had been at their mother's side when she passed on.
Her eyes had come to rest on K, and remained there when the doctor pronounced her dead. Like someone with a sleep disorder, asleep
with her eyes open. His weeping sister asked K to close her eyes. K
couldn't understand—she was already sleeping the deep sleep of the

dead, how could closing her eyelids make her any more comfortable? Why not simply leave her be? But he closed her eyes nonetheless. He remembered the last thing his sister had said:

"Good night, Mom. Sleep well."

And down went the curtain on the play titled *Family*. The women who had played the roles of Mom and Sister removed their makeup and disappeared. The applause that had filled the theater faded, and here was K, having scanned the photos in the program, having lunch with the actress playing Sister.

The noodles were tasty and K finished his bowl. His sister for her part ate instead the pastries K had brought; she had already finished the cake.

She'll weigh three hundred before long, then four-fifty—she won't be able to get up by herself or walk.

"You know, I'm sorry about last time."

By now K was wondering if his sister had dementia.

"I'd just remarried, and my second husband wasn't very well off—he was in real estate, property leases—and we were just scraping by. But he was like a godsend at the time. I had to support myself as a karaoke coach—that shows you how hard up I was. And that's when I got your letter."

"The letter?"

"The one you sent me?"

"I did?"

"Yes, the letter you sent to me."

K had never sent a letter to his sister. Their relationship was distant by then—he didn't know her phone number or where she lived—how could he have sent her a letter?

"I still have that letter. It's the only one I ever got from you."

"Do you mind if I smoke?" asked K.

"As long as I can have one too."

K searched his pockets, felt something he didn't recognize. The business card from the designated driver last night. He put it back in his pocket, located his cigarettes, and he and his sister lit up.

"You were practically begging me, but like I just said, I was not very well off then, and I couldn't help you out. I'm sorry, K."

It was the first time that day that she'd called him by name.

K concentrated, trying to recall *her* name. But not until she produced the letter did he remember. There it was, written on the envelope—KJS. K was their family name, no problem there, but JS? It
wasn't familiar. But that was her name all right, and the handwriting
was K's. However skillful a forger you might be, you couldn't fake
another person's handwriting any more accurately than you could
forge a fingerprint.

K had never written a letter to his sister. And yet here before
his eyes was such a letter, a letter bearing his handwriting. His sister removed the letter from the envelope and unfolded it. Two pages
from a notebook, the writing filling the front and back of each. This
handwriting too, obviously his.

"'It's been a while, Sister,'" she read, in between puffs on her
cigarette, her tone that of her heyday as an actress. "'How have you
been? I've been wanting to write but I never did. I'm sorry, Sister.
YD must be a big boy now, fourth or fifth grade, right?'"

YD—that's right, that was his name.

"'I guess I haven't been a very good uncle…'"

K didn't like any of this. If the handwriting was a hundred
percent his, the manner of expression was zilch. It sounded like
the consolatory letters schoolchildren wrote for homework to soldiers they had never met. K hated any kind of phony expression. It
sounded to him like the empty promises made by scheming politi-
cians at election time.

"You wouldn't happen to have any aspirin, would you?" he
asked JS, wanting a break from her monologue and recalling the
two pharmacies that were closed that day.

JS paused. "Not feeling well?"

"My ankle."

"You fell?"

"Well, actually," K began. He needed to try a little shock
treatment to sidetrack his sister. "I got bitten by a puppy."

"You did? Let's have a look."

She came up so close to K her bosom bumped into his face.
She bent over and removed his socks. His ankle was still an angry
red and still swollen. The wound was leaking into the gauze ban-
dage.

"My my my," she said as she prodded K over to the couch. "You need a disinfectant, not a painkiller. And the best way to disinfect is to suck out. Just like you suck the poison from a snake bite, you suck the bad stuff out from a dog bite. You never know what kind of germs are in a dog's mouth."

JS put her mouth to K's ankle, like a lifeguard giving artificial respiration. And began sucking on K's unwashed ankle. The suction of her mouth felt as strong as a vacuum cleaner's. K was perplexed—it was so sudden, so aggressive. In spite of himself he tried to wiggle free of JS's osculation.

"Sit still," said JS. "If you don't get rid of the bad stuff, you might get rabies." And in a sacrificial posture she sucked away at the puppy bite, as if it was the least she could do for him after declining the request in the letter, the exact nature of which still eluded K. Her lips were firmly attached, her tongue licking vigorously at the affected area. Her tongue licked vigorously at the affected area. So consumed was she that her bottom heaved like the buttocks in the close-up of the video clip on K's cell phone. From the rear she looked like she was performing fellatio on him.

Once when K was young he had cut himself trying to sharpen a pencil. JS had rushed to him saying, "Blood is too precious to waste—you have to suck it up."

K wondered now if she had developed a fetish for blood when she was girl, if she was a hematophiliac. Or a vampire.

Just then he felt a bolt of energy, a violent frenzy he had experienced before. Like magma in a volcano, steaming and bubbling and about to erupt in fiery plumes, like the earth trembling and about to split open when the volcano implodes. Like the suspense just before orgasm, pleasure accompanying self-reproach and a sense of primal sin, the instinctive fear in response to the sorrowful, dreary void following ejaculation. He wondered for a moment whether these myriad emotions were what he would feel if he had to be circumcised. And then a shudder ran through him and he felt an erection.

No, I can't. He shook his head. *In my mind It's incest, for Christ's sake.* He gritted his teeth. *Sister, JS, that's enough.* And he tensed all over, the sudden movement detaching her lips.

"Sister, I think that's enough. And I need to be going." To conceal his arousal, K put his socks back on, briskly retrieved his coat from the hanger, then rolled his pants legs down.

"All right, then, don't forget these," said his sister as she handed him the shopping bag with the parka and pants. "I won't be needing these. You can give them to your daughter."

K eyed the letter on the dining table. "Could I take this? I promise to return it along with the photos."

"Sure, go ahead."

"So long. And let's keep in touch and get together now and then."

And K meant it. He had to continue these occasional get-togethers — even though they were originally H's idea — if he was to recover his identity.

"All right, goodbye." At the door his sister embraced him. "*Aigo*, you little brat. See you next time."

On his way down the staircase K came across a family of mice. There must have been a dozen of them. They scurried off at his approach. He seemed to recall reading that this was a sign of an impeding earthquake. But why should they be concerned about an earthquake? He still felt the molten rock bubbling away inside him. And just as molten rock will burst through the weakest part of the earth's crust, the force churning inside K would bore away like a rock drill at the weakest, most sensitive part of his crust — his genitalia.

2:47 p.m.

It being Sunday, Campus Boulevard was closed to traffic. K would have to find a detour. But first he needed to relieve himself, so when he arrived at the boulevard he found a place to pull over. He spotted a coffee shop, rushed inside, and hurried to the men's room. As he tried to relieve himself, he realized that the urge he'd felt in the car was actually the magma-like surge of energy stirring inside him. He still had an erection. If not for what had just happened at his sister's, he would have marked it up as an aftereffect of last night's blue pill.

Finishing his business, K drank a coffee. The more he thought about it, the angrier he became. How could he have felt sexual desire for JS, his own sister? Even if you didn't classify his feelings as lust, wasn't the erection an obvious indication? *I'm a rutting animal, nothing but.*

Animals mate with their kin. But K wasn't an animal, he was human, and didn't humans have the capacity for reasoning? Among humans, incest was taboo, a boundary not to be crossed. In the Bible, when God condemned the cities of Sodom and Gomorrah he instructed righteous Lot's wife not to look back upon those cities, and when she contravened His order she turned into a pillar of salt. Lot's two daughters were left to care for him, and to address the critical matter of the lack of a male heir they plied Lot with wine and lay with him in succession, receiving his seed. Each daughter had a son by her father. And so the two boys were their father's sons and the daughters' younger brothers, and the daughters were both the boys' mothers and their older sisters, a confounding of normal blood relationships. Would you then call Lot a sinner, one who had abandoned principle? But wasn't righteous Lot the only person who avoided God's punishment?

K was all too aware that he was not a righteous man. Still, why the violent burst of magmatic lust he had felt for his sister, whom he hadn't seen in ten years? The tingling sensation was still there, the sensation of her sucking lips and clinging tongue, a brand on his body he could never remove. He had a sip of coffee and moaned in spite of himself, had another sip and felt the pounding of his heart.

High on the wall in the mostly empty coffee shop was a television where a news special was playing out, the two anchors, a man and a woman, reporting in turn on last night's earthquake near the West Sea. The quake had occurred at 2 a.m., and its 5.6 rating made it the most powerful earthquake in the nation's history. Stark images of the damage on the island near the epicenter were visible on the screen. The devastation was unimaginable — houses in ruins, utility poles toppled, fires burning, some twenty people dead, and the injured still being accounted for but thought to number one hundred. What caught K's eye were not the scenes of devastation but an image of fish flopping in a yard. Here was one more irony of the cruel tragicomedy that was human life—the earthquake had endangered the lives of hundreds, while its tremors yielded a similar number of fish caught without the aid of a net.

The male anchor man passed the microphone to his colleague, who explained that the earthquake was thought to be a precursor to a stronger one, and although Seoul appeared to be far enough from the epicenter it was connected to it by fault lines and therefore people should be vigilant. The quake had resulted from a high-pressure magma reservoir breaching a weak point in the ocean floor.

The anchor woman, she had a familiar face. Not the face that was part of the composite he saw anchoring the evening news. Rather it was the face itself; it was the déjà vu face of the woman with the butterfly tattoo from last night, and earlier in the day, that of the spread-legged exhibitionist-cum-stinky woman he had brushed past outside the café. The camera occasionally zoomed in on the anchor woman's face—yes, it was her, no doubt about it. So now she was playing the role of anchor. But how was she able to appear at the bar, at the café, and on the TV screen all at the same time?

Well, it was possible if they were all duplicates. Extract a somatic cell from one person, transfer the nucleus of that cell to an egg from which the nucleus has been removed, and you have yourself a person with the same genetic composition—in other words, a clone. Already there was Dolly the Sheep, and cloned rodents would soon follow. And here at home haven't we already cloned a cow?

K asked if it was all right to smoke. Yes, he was told, as long as he went outside. So out he went to a table with a patio umbrella and pots of chrysanthemums. He felt better out here—it was an exhilarating autumn day.

K lit up and watched the dating couples promenading along the pedestrians-only boulevard. A soccer ball was being kicked around. A bare-chested foreigner was drinking beer and singing. And then K noticed the woman in the maxi coat walking among the foreigners in his direction. The coat was familiar and K placed it immediately. He experienced a lethargic dizziness, wondered for a moment if he was about to have a seizure. Ants build up their ant-hills before it rains, mice band together before an earthquake—K too had developed this sixth sense, a miraculous dispensation of nature in addition to the inborn five senses, a deep-seated instinctual capacity. This "over-sense" always started with an awareness that something was familiar.

K zeroed in on the woman. It wasn't just her coat, but also the black dress, the hairstyle, the way she walked—everything about her was familiar. She was yesterday's exhibitionist and butterfly-tattooed woman and today's news anchor. And now she was homing in on K, but trying to remain anonymous. Had she lined him up in her sights? K went on the defensive. And then the clone brushed past him. The smell—yes, it was the stinky odor from yesterday.

What to make of this weird phenomenon? Per H's diagnosis he had met his sister for the first time in ten years and now felt sure his sister was real, just as her photo album told him his mother was real. And this awareness told him his own existence was real and not a mock experiment, not the pseudo-reality of a simulation. And yet the reality all about him was still reversed, disjointed, awry, warped, and confused.

K turned away from the sun that was hitting him full in the face and toward the shade of the umbrella. As he did so he noticed inside the coffee shop a woman sitting at the window. K's sixth sense cast its net. The woman who had just brushed past him, she was now in the very place he had sat. She didn't try to avoid his gaze but looked straight at him, declaring her presence. Their eyes met and deliberately she unbuttoned her coat, displaying her chest. K was now the only person who could see her head. Ten feet and a pane of glass were all that separated them. Nonchalantly the woman undid the top button of her blouse, showing her neck. *Go right ahead, I'm not going to let you stare me down.* She freed button number two, revealing the deep valley between her large breasts, and began fingering button number three. It had almost popped free when a man barged in and sat down beside her.

K couldn't overhear them but they appeared to be lovers. The man had sculpted good looks. Something about him was familiar. Was he that clone of a man K had seen with the exhibitionist woman at the café yesterday? He couldn't say for sure, he'd only seen that man from the rear. But this man was familiar, and now K knew—he was a clone of his sister-in-law's new husband. He had the same naked brazenness, the same confidence, a man who had made dozens of journeys to the altar. Did that mean he had stolen away from his wife during their honeymoon in Bali and caught a flight back home? Impossible unless he was a time traveler. But if he was a clone—now *that* opened up all sorts of possibilities. Clone A could be in Bali while clone B was on a date here on Campus Boulevard with clone D. What's more, the coffee they were drinking could be a Clone Drip and the coffee shop mock reality, a simulation, a laboratory.

The woman resumed her exhibition. The man's arrival seemed to have pumped up the thrill of unsealing herself to K. Her crimson tongue sucked at her lip, reminding K of JS's tongue, and in no time he was aroused. The woman, still fingering button number three of her blouse, undid it as artfully as a pickpocket. The silk blouse began to slither down her shoulders, and just as deftly she arrested the slide. She exhibited a lady's primness but her make-believe bashfulness merely camouflaged her shedding act. By now her braless bosom was exposed except for the nipples. She was a seasoned strip-teaser, a call girl-cum-exotic dancer offering voyeuristic arousal inside her glass booth, an elaborate carnal display in which she peeled away her clothing with hands as dexterous as as a chef's fruit knives.

What came next was astonishing—her hand crept to the man's and eased it inside her clothing. The man and woman looked at each other and flashed a grin—the man had been expecting this. His hand beneath the blouse began working like fingers on a keyboard. The caresses excited them until they came together in a kiss, unmindful of others. The back of the man's head covered her face, but only up to the eyes, which once again held K's gaze. Her eyes should have been closed in the passion of the kiss, but here they were again, like at the café yesterday, engaging K in a staredown. Her lips were kissing the man but her eyes were kissing K. K felt like he'd come across a swingers' party.

Just then K's cell phone vibrated. It was a text message. *Want more?* Was it the woman? No, it couldn't be. He hadn't seen her either texting or speaking on a cell phone. It must have been spam—one of those texts winging in several times a day, mostly from lenders but including the occasional sex trade come-on. *If so, call us.* Hmm—and a phone number too. What a coincidence. K closed the phone and placed it on the table.

And then he noticed the business card—the one left by the designated driver last night. K had stuck it in the pocket containing his cigarettes, inadvertently inserting it inside the cellophane of the pack. He removed the card and studied it. Instead of the driver's name it bore a photo of a nude woman and the following:

> *Are You Lonesome Tonight?*
> *Come Visit Our Luxury Girls*
> *Yŏksam Adult Club*
> *35 minutes—40,000 wŏn * 60 minutes—70,000 wŏn*

Followed by English:

> *Membership Only. 100% Reservation.*
> *Open 11 am to 6 am, 365 Everyday.*

K turned the card over; this side was in English only:

> *The Club and Manager Service.*
> *Sweetheart Mood. Kiss, Hug, Talk, Event, Party.*
> *Telephone: xxx-xxxx-xxxx*

The phone number looked familiar. K reopened his phone, called up the text he'd just received, checked the phone number. Up it came on the screen. Same as the phone number on the card.

He hadn't received it at random, he'd been chosen. Nor was the timing of the message random. The sender had been able to target, with more accuracy than a satellite, the time K could be found here on Campus Boulevard at this coffee shop—twenty three minutes and fifteen seconds past the hour of three, by K's watch, on Sunday afternoon. Yesterday it had been the exhibitionist and the woman with the butterfly tattoo, but today it was her reincarnation, the television anchor, who was initiating the contact, at a time when K would be here at the coffee shop. What's more, the designated driver, and his predecessor, party B, had been able to predict where K would be twenty-four hours later, and during that time had not relaxed their surveillance for a moment. And K's visit to his sister, JS? A decoy instituted by all of them—they had obviously coerced H into making that suggestion to K. And for all he knew, the volcanic lust he'd felt toward JS was the result of a drug they'd slipped him.

Now he knew. Every train station displays a timetable. Barring something unusual, the trains leave and arrive according to schedule. For the public it's a kind of civic contract, it's the way things work. Likewise, weren't all of K's thoughts and actions following a sequence, a meticulous computerized program? Hadn't K become a human train, an automaton, coming and going as programmed? If he wanted to try a different kind of coffee, wouldn't that thought too have been programmed by Big Brother? And even if he were to select orange juice instead of coffee in an attempt to circumvent Big Brother's control, wouldn't such a niggling deviation also be consistent with Big Brother's plan?

Not for a minute, not by an inch, could K escape remote control by this transcendent being. Therefore he had to call the number on the business card and make a reservation to kiss and hug and enjoy the sweetheart mood at the Adult Club. It was an order from the guiding hand, part of a timetable he could not ignore. It was like the brew with which K had been injected to arouse his violent lust for JS, like the wine with which the daughters of Lot had plied their father before they lay with him to receive his seed. The guiding hand that had worked through the original sin of incest had passed the baton to K so that the human race would continue to reproduce and not go extinct.

He had to make the call; he could not disobey this order from the here and now. The magma inside him was bubbling away thanks to the preview through the coffee shop window. Who knew when it would erupt?

He looked again through that window. The man and woman were gone. While K was distracted, the two secret envoys had discharged their roles and vanished like a mirage. And now they were offstage, waiting for the next act.

K entered the number from the business card.

"Hello." An instant response.

"Is this the club?"

"Yes, it is." The man at the other end spoke in a clipped military tone.

"I'd like to make a reservation."

"Sunday is always busy for us—what time would you prefer?"

"First could you tell me where you're located?"

"It's a five-minute walk from Kangnam Station."

"In that case, let's make it four thirty?"

"How about four forty-five—we'll have more time to work with."

"Fine," said K.

"And were you thinking of thirty-five minutes or sixty? Or you could make a longer reservation, at double the price."

"Could I make that decision once I get there?"

"Certainly, sir. Please plan to arrive at Kangnam Station, exit number four, by four thirty-five, and I will call you at this number. Welcome to our club, sir—you are now a member. Your membership number is the last four digits of your phone number—five one one zero. And that is how we will address you—'Member Five One One Zero.' This is your own personal ID number, and with it you may enjoy your session assured of absolute privacy."

It all sounded prerecorded.

"We can also arrange for a business trip."

"I see."

K closed the phone and left the coffee shop. He felt like a special agent charged with a secret mission.

4:32 p.m.

The Kangnam subway station was located in the heart of the New Seoul, south of the Han River, a strategic transportation center bearing a chaotic flood of people. Even so, exit four was not difficult to find. K was bearing down on it along the underground shopping arcade when his cell phone sounded. He answered the call in stride.

"It's me." It was his wife. And then the standard question: "Where are you?"

"Kangnam Station—I'm meeting someone."

"I'm spending the evening with my mother—I don't think I can attend Mass. She's feeling lonely, so I should probably look after her. MS is with me, so you can go to Mass by yourself. And if you can take care of your dinner, that would be nice."

"Don't worry, I'll be fine."

An FYI call. K said goodbye. He realized now that the 6:30 Mass was the real reason he had blurted out 4:30 on the phone; the travel time between Campus Boulevard and Kangnam Station was not the issue. That way, whether he booked thirty-five or sixty minutes at the club, he could finish by 5:30 and be at the at church on time.

Outside, the sky had clouded over. A fierce gust of wind battered the streetside trees, leaving a whirl of leaves along the pavement. Diagonally across from him was a tall building with a huge video screen that became brighter and sharper as the skies grew cloudier. The special report on the earthquake was still in progress. From high up on the building the female anchor, formerly the exhibitionist and the woman with the butterfly tattoo, and now cloned into the coffee shop woman, kept a watchful eye on K.

From a flowerbed near the exit a pack of rats darted onto the sidewalk, heedless of human gazes, and scattered, leaving a trail of squealing women running pell-mell in every direction.

K leaned back against the railing at the top of the exit stairs and from deep underground felt a slight tremor. Another earthquake? But the next moment he realized it was the subway passing beneath him.

His cell phone sounded. K answered.

"Is this member 5110?" The familiar voice of the man at the club.

"Yes."

"Here are the directions; please listen carefully. You're just outside exit four, correct?"

"Yes."

"Then do you see S Building across the street?"

K saw it. It being the weekend, the interior was only partially lit, the lighted windows like clusters of grapes.

"Yes, I see it."

"All right, stay on your side of the street but continue downhill, keeping that building in sight. Go straight past an alley on your right, and at the first intersection turn right. A hundred yards down that street you'll see B Officetel on your left. Go up to the eighth floor, find suite 119, and press the doorbell."

"All right."

Following the man's directions, K walked down the main street past the alley and arrived at the intersection. He turned right, passed an alley chock-full of eateries, and came out at another intersection. To the left was a building he took to be the officetel. He walked like a robot, feeling like a wind-up toy soldier that hits a wall, bounces off, and marches off in the opposite direction.

Suddenly he felt a chill—capricious fall weather with its winds. He entered the officetel lobby and was glad for its warmth. The elevator was off to the side. Just then a man brushed past him. He looked familiar, but K couldn't place him and gave him no further thought.

The elevator arrived and its occupants surged out. They too looked familiar. *Did I see them somewhere?* But the next moment they were out of sight and out of mind.

A few others joined K, each looking familiar, and up went the elevator. One of the walls was glass, and outside, the giant video display looked even brighter in the approaching dusk. The female anchor was still there. The familiar passengers got out at their respective floors, and finally K arrived at the eighth floor.

He found himself before a sign with two fingers, one pointing left for suites 101-110 and the other pointing right for 111-120. He went right and stopped at number 119. The remains of several take-out meals were piled outside the door. He pressed the bell, but there was no immediate response. A peephole lens was mounted in the middle of the door. Again he pressed the bell, and this time the door opened, but only wide enough to show a man's face. A metal chain spanned the opening.

"Who is it?"

"A member." K paused. "Member 5110."

The door opened the rest of the way. The man welcomed K inside—he must be the manager. K saw a narrow hallway with doors on both sides. Closer by was a reception counter and next to it a small couch where a man sat reading a book. K had seen the man somewhere but couldn't place him—he was beginning to feel like an amnesiac. But no need to dwell on the man.

"Please have a seat, sir."

K sat. Two people made the couch feel cramped. The other man glanced at K. He might have been the father-in-law from yesterday's wedding who had become the brother-in-law at JS's apartment, he could have been a clone, or he could simply be someone who bore a resemblance to them—K couldn't be sure.

A man appeared from the far end of the hall. He walked up to the counter looking like he'd just finished a hearty meal, produced his wallet and paid, then departed. K thought of a car cruising in, low-fuel warning light gleaming on the instrument display, and getting refueled before gliding off.

"This way, please," said the manager to the other man. The man closed his book and scurried off after the manager. This time K imagined a man with an aching tooth hurrying into the dentist's office.

K looked up at the clock. It read 4:50—already five minutes late. He picked up the book the man had been reading. *Sailor Moon, the Moon Nymph*—a comic book featuring miniskirt-clad girls in sailor tunics. K remembered seeing them in a cartoon show long ago. But he wasn't really interested in graphic novels and such, so he put the book aside and looked about.

In the small space the half-dozen doors resembled phone booths. The space was so small that the half-dozen doors resembled phone booths. Small spaces for short-term pleasure, K decided. Each of those rooms must be occupied. A dozen people all told in this suite, but you couldn't even hear a person breathing. Did that mean the place was soundproofed? No way. But then where did all the sounds go—there was no moaning, no creaking of a bed, no swishing sounds of movement, no stifled coughing or sneezing. The silence was oppressive and ominous. There was a dead feeling to the place, as if it had been visited by something evil. And in that silence, familiar men and unfamiliar women were in the "sweetheart mood," indulging in "kiss," "hug," "talk," "event," and "party." Silent kissing, silent talking, silent sex.

Men kissing, hugging, whispering to unknown women they've never seen before, whose warmth they've never felt, women they've never spoken with. *I love you*—pleading, appealing, screaming, wailing—a burning thirst, a wanting, a lack, a hurt, a soundless outcry. Like performing artificial respiration, restarting the lungs, bringing back to life a nearly drowned body from familiar waters. Like an intravenous tube bringing nourishment to an anorexic at the point of starvation. Relationships, understanding, escape from oppression, confirmation of existence, liberation and freedom, and on the other hand darkness, sin and evil, masochism, nihilism, despair, violence, destruction, and suicidal acts.

And then the manager reappeared.

"This way, please."

K followed the manager into a bathroom only large enough for a toilet and sink. A new toothbrush and toothpaste lay on the washstand beneath the mirror.

"If you would, sir," said the man as he handed the items to K. "And for your information," he continued, as if reading from a primer, "when you kiss, you are allowed to feel outside the clothing, bosom, buttocks, anywhere—the finishing touch is left to the member. But if a hand goes inside the skirt, if bare flesh is felt, if any attempt is made to remove the clothing, if violence is employed or forcible sex attempted, an alarm will sound and the member will be escorted from the premises."

K could only nod, his mouth full of foaming toothpaste.

The man continued reading from his instruction manual: "As explained, the base rate is 40,000 for 35 minutes, and for an hour it will be an additional 30,000."

K continued to brush his teeth, his eyes on the mirror.

"And finally, there is no refund. Do you have any questions?"

K shook his head and the man left.

K rinsed his mouth and for good measure washed his hands

and face. He returned to the waiting area to find a new arrival, a man sitting on the couch and trimming his fingernails.

"This way, sir," said the manager to K. K followed the man to the room at the end of the hall. Inside was a space just large enough to accommodate a couch just long enough for a person to lie down on. The room was musty. There being no window, there was probably no air circulation either.

There was a timer on a shelf; the manager wound it. "After 30 minutes the timer goes off. You may decide then if you wish to extend. If you press this button, you will be connected to reception."

K took a seat on the couch and inspected the room. The shelf contained Handi-Wipes and a roll of toilet paper. One wall was taken up by a mirror, inviting the customer to view all of his antics, functioning like a kaleidoscope.

Suddenly there was a woman opposite the door. It registered to K that the customer and the woman arrived by separate entrances. No, he couldn't call her a woman, she was a girl—that's what shocked him. But the next moment he realized this was an illusion, an illusion created by her appearance, starting with her hair, which was bright yellow, and the white gloves that extended above her elbows. She wore an English-style sailor's tunic with a red ribbon that dwarfed her bosom. Her pleated skirt was so short it revealed her bottom. She wore white knee-length boots that, because of their lacing, would take forever to remove, the laces bunched together like the legs of a centipede. The getup was that of an anime character rather than an actual person. She was dressed the same as the character in *Sailor Moon, the Moon Nymph*, the comic book on the couch in the reception area.

The girl sat down next to K and smiled. "Hello, Mister," she said in a singsong voice. Her tone was very familiar—it was his daughter's customary greeting to him. And now that he saw the woman close up, he realized it was not only her costume that was girlish but also her face—no makeup, not a wrinkle in sight, the skin firm and elastic.

K hesitated before responding. "How old are you, miss?'

"How old do I look?"

"You look underage."

"Well, I'm not," she simpered. "Want to see my ID?"

"What's your name."

"Sailor Moon," she said, indicating the red ribbon over her chest. "Sailor Moon, the Moon Nymph." Her voice hummed, making her sound more like a doll than a person. And the rest of her as well looked more like a "real doll" than a person, a fine life-size silicone sex doll with movie makeup, a doll specially made to mimic the movements of the human body—wrists, knees, everything.

K felt her shoulder. She was human all right but the flesh felt like silicone—K imagined synthetically enlarged breasts.

"Want something, sir?" said Sailor Moon, displaying her tongue and sucking on it. Then she added in English, "Hug? Kiss? Talk? Event?"

Costume play—K had read about it in a magazine. Shortened to *cosplay* by the new generation, with whom it was popular. In real life you role-play anime or video game characters; it had developed into a craze among young people.

I came all the way here for an anime character, Sailor Moon, the Moon Nymph.

In her gloved hand was a wand somewhat longer than a candy-on-a-stick and studded with faux gemstones. The wand came to rest on K's lips and then his chest and then his nether regions.

"Magical Sailor Moon—transform into the Moon Nymph."

"What's that?" said K.

"It's a magic wand. Go like this," she said, stroking him with the wand, "and it makes miracles. I'm making you and me into soldiers."

"Soldiers?"

"Soldiers of earth, soldiers of the future. You'll be Leon, Knight of the White Rose, and I'll be the guardian soldier of the Tree of Life."

"The Tree of Life?"

"Mister, you want to *talk* instead of *kiss*, right?" said Sailor Moon, cupping K's face tenderly. Her lips came close to K's, then met them firmly. And with all the expertise of a drill sergeant training a raw recruit, she inserted her tongue into K's mouth. It was a sweet sensation. But then Sailor Moon, professional at kissing that she was, withdrew and brought her mouth to K's ear. K felt her hot breath.

"Together we protect the Tree of Life," she murmured.

"What do you mean, Tree of Life?" All K could do was ask questions.

"The Tree of Life takes care of people on earth. Ann and Allen, the evil ones, want to kill it. The only way to keep it alive is through the power of earthlings—that's the only way to save it."

The Tree of Life—the only way to save earth, the tree that this girl, transformed into Sailor Moon, will protect. Did she mean the apple tree, which the biblical Creator made, the apple being the fruit of good or evil? K recalled the passage where the Creator appoints Adam, the first human He created, guardian of the Garden of Eden, commanding him to eat the fruit of any tree he wishes, with the exception of the tree of good and evil, and if he should eat the fruit of the tree of good and evil, verily on that day shall he perish. Eve, tempted by the serpent, fed Adam the fruit of that tree, and that original sin resulted in humanity's loss of eternal life and fall from grace. "From dust to dust," spoke the Creator, and true to his words, humanity became dust. We're about to lose the Tree of Life. The Tree of Life on earth, which Sailor Moon, the Moon Nymph, is trying to save. Isn't that the Tree of Life that the Creator made?

"Want to hear the song Sailor Moon sings to save the Tree of Life?" she asked in a dulcet voice as she caressed K's face with her wand. Without waiting for his response she began to sing:

I'm sorry I'm not being honest,
But if this is a dream,
I would ease up to you
And confess all.
On nights I cannot call you,
My fluttering heart
Is called by the moonlight
To the magical fairyland
Where our dreamlike love
Shines far into the night sky.

How lucid and pure her voice was—the *sweetheart mood* of a nocturnal serenade outside one's window. The song continued:

> *It is not by chance*
> *That I meet you, my dear,*
> *Among the countless stars*
> *For I am your Magical Sailor Moon.*

Her song concluded, Sailor Moon found K's lips once more and murmured, "Leon, Knight of the White Rose, meeting you like this is not an accident. I, Magical Sailor Moon, am looking for a brave soldier to save the Tree of Life. Mister Leon, let's be soldiers for the future."

"So what do I do to be Leon?"

"You keep coming back. You ask for the same manager. You keep your eyes off the other girls. You only ask for Sailor Moon. You and me, close as we can be. Promise." To seal the deal she offered her pinky for K to link his with.

K made no response. He had no mind to become the Knight of the White Rose, no courage to save the Tree of Life on earth, no sense of mission. Maybe Shim Ch'ŏng could do it—after all she had thrown herself into the Indang Sea as a sacrifice so her blind father could recover his sight, but K was too old to transform into a cartoon figure like Sailor Moon and enter an anime reality to save the earth.

Still, Sailor Moon took K's pinky in hers, bumped thumbs with him, and chanted: "Under the sky, under the stars, you and me, pinky swear!" And finally the triple spit to seal the promise.

Just then the timer went off. From a speaker came the manager's voice: "Thirty minutes are up. What will it be, sir?"

K heard Sailor Moon's sultry voice close to his ear: "Tell him an hour. I like you, Sir Leon. You're not a dirty old man or a sex maniac. And don't listen to what he says, you can feel under my skirt anywhere you want. And my boobs too."

"What will it be, sir?" The voice was more pressing.

"The whole hour," said K.

"Yes, sir." The intercom went silent.

Sailor's Moon's lips found K's and fastened on to them. It felt like JS sucking on his ankle. And the magma began bubbling once more, pushing toward the weak point in K's crust. Sailor Moon's lips took the place of JS's. K let out a moan like a torture victim who has just been broken.

Please. He was panting. *Please, don't. I don't want this.*

6:03 p.m.

K arrived at the church 30 minutes early. Two men and a woman were waiting their turn at the confessional. Preparing to confess, they scanned the stream of arrivals for the evening Mass, cognizant of their gazes. On the other hand, they looked proud of their steely faith, which prompted them to confess the puniest of sins. The booth was both a launderette for cleaning the soul and a high court for the invisible controlling hand. K wondered if in his role as deputy of the Creator as well as junior Big Brother, the father confessor felt fear, like a defendant awaiting a judge's sentence. A passage from the Bible had been posted outside the box to ease troubled minds:

"The son said, 'Father, I have sinned, against God and against you; I am no longer fit to be called your son; treat me as one of your paid servants.' But the father said to his servants, 'Quick! Fetch a robe, my best one, and put it on him; put a ring on his finger and shoes on his feet. Bring the fatted calf and kill it, and let us have a feast to celebrate the day. For this son of mine was dead and has come back to life; he was lost and was found.'"

K recognized the story of the prodigal son. So if he were to sin against his father and then confess that sin and ask forgiveness, would his father be so overjoyed he would welcome him back with a feast? *Have I sinned?* K asked himself, and while he wondered he took his place in line behind the two men and the woman. *I am a descendant of the first man, who ate of the fruit of good and evil, and his genes are within me. Apart from that original sin, is there a sin I should be confessing? Was it a sin to give Sailor Moon, the Moon Nymph, 70,000 wŏn for making out and feeling her up?*

K had lingered in that cubbyhole for forty-five minutes. And yet he had paid for an hour, refusing the manager's offer of a 10,000-*wŏn* discount. He had also given Sailor Moon a 10,000-*wŏn* tip. K shouldn't have been throwing his money around, but that tip was the least he could do on behalf of the worthy cause of saving the Tree of Life. No way could that money be considered payment for a sexual transaction, an act of prostitution. He wasn't buying Sailor Moon's body. From the menu he had ordered *kiss, hug,* and *sweetheart*—an à la carte feel-up, not the buffet. The flaring of carnal magma at JS's apartment had not erupted with Sailor Moon. In the end, K had been a dud and Sailor Moon a "real doll." She was an abstract being, a Pinocchio-like figure existing only within the comic book panels, with whom sexual contact was possible only in the realm of anime. And for that he had sinned?

No, the reason for the anomaly that was K's imminent confession was his compulsion for JS. JS was his sister—a fact he had confirmed beyond a shadow of a doubt. And by confirming her existence and that of his mother, he was able to verify his own identity. But his encounter with his sister had spurred that magmatic lust. However he conceptualized it—carnal desire, debauchery—it was an experience no less fierce than that of the first woman, who, lured by the snake, looked upon the tree of the knowledge of good and evil and thought how fresh and delicious its fruit looked. The urge for that fruit was forbidden. And K's coveting his blood sister was unforgivable, a sin of which he stood guilty. Didn't the Bible say that whosoever harbors lewd thoughts toward a woman has committed adultery in his mind, that if the right eye sins one must pluck it out? K couldn't explain his urge for JS, but his thoughts were filthy and lustful, that much was clear. In his mind he had sinned against his sister. It was an immoral act for which he would be cast into hell.

Of the three people K had found awaiting confession there remained only one of the men. He was an elderly, bespectacled gentleman with a mild manner. K wondered if he was a retired principal. The man held a rosary, his hand trembling faintly. What sin could this sterling gentleman have committed? Was he, contrary to his looks, a scheming con artist? Was he, unbeknown to his wife, a skirt chaser? Was he a professional thief? Was he feeling so guilty that his hand was trembling?

And the person now in the booth, a woman of early middle age, what sin was she confessing to the priest? With her lavish fur and elaborate makeup, K had no doubt she was rich. What sin could she have committed? K imagined her face imprinted with the scarlet letter, like hoarded wealth stamped for confiscation by the tax collector. Was she a conniving adulterer, a fetus killer, guilty of both a sin and a crime?

The confessional box consisted of three booths in front and three in back. But so few parishioners partook of the sacrament that the booths in back were not in use. The booths that were in use were identified by a sensor light above the entrance. When a person entered, the light went on; when the occupant emerged, it went off. The priest sat between the double array of booths and could hear a confession from either side.

The light over one of the booths went out and the woman in fur emerged. She was dabbing at her eyes with a handkerchief. Why was she crying—from the relief of unburdening herself? From pride for having undergone penance? From an overwhelming surge of emotion? Before long she had returned to her pew. The gentleman entered the same booth and the light went on.

K would be next. In the meantime two later arrivals had taken their places behind him. One was a spiffed-up corporate type, the other a high school girl in her uniform. The girl resembled Sailor Moon, the Moon Nymph. But Sailor Moon would still be working, so it most certainly was not her.

K began to feel anxious. Not about the sin he would confess, but because he couldn't think of the proper procedure. He rarely undertook the sacrament of holy confession. He felt obligated to do so at Easter and Christmas, but what he confessed on those occasions you would be hard pressed to call a sin. Indeed, in his mind he was free of sin. He believed in none other than the Creator, the unseen hand, and he did not worship idols. He observed the Sabbath faithfully, and not once had he sullied it. He was not a vulgar philistine. Never had he committed adultery, never had he lied, never had he coveted another man's wife or assets.

He was especially steadfast about not lying. It was not that he didn't lie; rather, he didn't know how to lie. In primary school he hadn't received the highest grades, but his homeroom teachers gave him high marks for honesty. So when out of a sense of duty he partook of confession, it was painful to come up with a sin to confess. Upright person that he was, he had no knack for fabrication. If you were a believer you had to abide by the commandments—in his mind it was simply the right thing to do.

And so what he confessed to was usually a lack of charity. He failed to bestow kindness upon others, for example, he neglected to contribute to their welfare, he was indifferent to volunteering, or serving, or inconveniencing himself for others. He justified his lack of interest in others by telling himself he shouldn't invade their privacy. The problem for K was the concept that an act of charity involving me and you, whether material or spiritual, meant there was no difference between you and me; which in turn meant that "I am you" and "you are me"—and to K that was a logical contradiction.

It was Easter when K had last undertaken the sacrament. He had confessed to the priest that he had sinned by showing no pity to others. This confession had come after a bout of hard thinking about the Last Supper and Jesus' teaching to those sitting to his right. Jesus had said, "When I was hungry you gave me food; when thirsty, you gave me drink; when I was a stranger you took me into your home… " And the righteous had replied, "Lord, when was it that we saw you hungry and fed you, or thirsty and gave you drink?" And Jesus had said, "I tell you this: anything you did for one of your brothers here, however humble, you did for me." If what Jesus had said was true, then K was not qualified to sit to the right of Jesus. Never had he given food to one who was hungry, never had he looked after one who was ill, never had he visited one who was imprisoned—he was a pitiless man. K did not consider lack of pity to be sinful, but Jesus had said it was so, and therefore K confessed his heartlessness to the priest.

K had never given food to the hungry, and never would he have accepted such help from others. He expected no care from others if he were to fall ill, would accept no sympathy from others in a time of need—such was his life philosophy. And so it was always abstractions to which K confessed, and never realities.

But... The gentleman emerged from the booth to the blinking of the light above, and K entered. *What I'm about to confess is surely a sin. If Jesus' teaching is correct, if to harbor lewd thoughts toward a woman is already to have sinned, then I have sinned greatly.*

K sank down on the kneeler and reviewed the Guide for Confession posted on the wall. In the middle of that wall was a small round lattice that allowed priest and penitent to converse without either face being visible. While K waited, he heard through the tiny apertures in the lattice the priest murmuring to a penitent in another booth.

K made the sign of the cross. He felt tense knowing that for the first time in his life he would confess to an actual sin. He imagined a niggardly peddler trying to exchange a defective item at a barter market.

He heard the lattice slat to the other booth clack shut, and the slat to his booth clack open, and then the muted voice of the priest.

"By the mercy and grace of God the father, repent ye of your sins and make a true confession. Amen."

"In the name of the Father, the Son, and the Holy Spirit, my last confession was seven or eight months ago, father. It was during Easter."

Although the priest seated in his compartment was not visible, K knew by the man's voice who he was—the head priest, an older man. And here he was before the start of Mass, hearing confession.

"You may confess," he said, coughing.

"Father, today I have sinned. For the first time in my life I went to a place of indecency, where sex may be bought, and there I hugged and kissed with a woman I don't know."

"And did you consummate the act?"

K did not immediately reply, wondering exactly what the priest meant. Again he heard the priest's hacking cough. "I did not engage in a sexual act... But I am guilty of a worse sin—today I saw my older sister for the first time in ten years, and I felt a desire for her. Whether it was sexual desire or some other urge I don't know, but there is no doubt in my mind that I experienced impure thoughts." To emphasize the point he added, "She is my blood sister." He said nothing further, self-conscious because it was unnecessary to have added this. He was a third-rate actor hamming it up and overdramatizing his performance. "Please forgive me as well for all the other sins I have committed."

There was no response from the priest other than his hacking. He must have caught a bad cold. He could be heard blowing his nose, and then his voice drew near the lattice.

"Do not chastise yourself, my brother. But pray to the Lord that you do not repeat such thoughts and actions, lest they become chronic. I grant you penance."

And that was that. What a surprise. Compared with the weight of the sin, the sentence was short and to the point. Were his sins not as weighty as he had thought? Or was the priest's cold so miserable that he was taking a shortcut?

"In atonement for your sins, read chapter eight of the Book of John and recite the Lord's Prayer three times." And then the priest murmured the absolution: "Almighty God, Father of mercy, through the death and the resurrection of His son, has reconciled the world to Himself and sent the Holy Spirit among us for the forgiveness of sins; through the ministry of the Church may God grant you pardon and peace, and in the name of the Father, the Son, and the Holy Spirit, I absolve you of your sins, amen."

"Amen," said K, making the sign of the cross.

"Pray thee to the Lord, who has forgiven you your sins. May you go in peace."

And then the slat clacked shut over the lattice.

"Thank you, father."

K emerged from the booth. The confession had taken only a few minutes. Could his sin be forgiven in such a short sacrament? Why couldn't they just stamp "Forgiven" on his palm or give him a "Remission of Sin" receipt.

He found the row containing his usual seat—it was the third row from the front, to the right of the central aisle. With the start of the Mass drawing near, the sanctuary was already full. The choir was rehearsing a hymn. In accordance with the penance prescribed by the priest, K closed his eyes and recited the Lord's Prayer. He felt like a fortune teller, or a magician casting a spell. He picked up the thick Bible from the receptacle in front of him, found John 8, and began reading.

…*the scribes and the Pharisees brought in to him a woman who had been caught in adultery. They made her stand before him and said, "Now, master, this woman has been caught in adultery, in the very act. According to the Law, Moses commanded us to stone such women. Now, what do you say about her?"*

They said this to test him, so that they might have some good grounds for an accusation. But Jesus stooped down and began to write with his finger in the dust on the ground. But as they persisted in their questioning, he straightened himself up and said to them, "Let the one among you who has never sinned throw the first stone at her." Then he stooped down again and continued writing with his finger on the ground. And when they heard what he said, they were convicted by their own consciences and went out, one by one, beginning with the eldest until they had all gone.

Jesus was left alone, with the woman still standing where they had put her. So he stood up and said to her, "Where are they all—did no one condemn you?"

K thought he understood why the priest had selected this passage for him to reflect upon. The woman had been caught in the act of adultery. She was an unchaste woman who, according to tribal law, could be stoned. Through a clever stratagem Jesus had saved the woman. "Neither do I condemn you," he said to her. "Go now and leave your life of sin." And so he forgave her. Like Jesus with the woman, the priest had not condemned K. Instead he had instructed him to read this biblical passage and not to repeat his sins lest they become chronic. The scene he had selected was almost cinematic, enhancing the effectiveness of his forgiveness.

K admired how Jesus had handled himself, and especially the way he had snared the scribes. Logically the scribes were the villains, but in refuting them—"let the one among you who has never sinned cast the first stone"—he had led them to acknowledge their own sins and to act on their conscience. K had seen so many people who were both sinful and criminal, people who had thrown rocks, hurled Molotov cocktails, launched tear gas canisters, set fires, shot others, commandeered aircraft and flown them into buildings, committed massacres, dropped nuclear bombs. But the villains in the Bible, hadn't they acknowledged their sins and withdrawn?

But for K the crux of that scene was Jesus' silence as he wrote on the ground while being questioned. What was he writing? The question nagged at K. Was he doodling? Was he sketching something? Or was he in a quandary as to an answer, pondering his next move? Or was he practicing his breathing exercises, a cunning example of psychological warfare, allowing him to earn time while he pacified a frenzied mob?

To K he was a master gambler, with a woman's life at stake. To the overconfident scribes with their full house he showed a poker face as he placed four aces on the table. K liked the idea of Jesus the gambler. He felt he was watching an electrifying thriller, a climactic scene from a Hitchcock film where the action is rocketing toward a reversal.

Finally the Mass commenced. The faithful rose and joined the choir in the opening hymn while the head priest, who in the name of the Holy Spirit had forgiven K of his sins, made his entrance and proceeded toward the altar followed by the curates and acolytes.

A soprano voice burst out behind K, singing an octave higher than the other voices. It was a beautiful voice, but too close for comfort and it irritated him. The anxious voice of a would-be diva whose career aspirations had been dealt an ignominious defeat. He stole a look over his shoulder and saw the woman from the confession booth. The woman registered K's gaze, mistook it for admiration of her splendid voice, and the next K knew, she had turned up the volume to forte. He considered moving, but the sanctuary was full—better to ride out the hymn. The soprano continued to be an annoyance throughout. Normally K enjoyed the service. At the library he was mindful of others, and in church he focused on the ceremony, concentrating the way a magnifying glass can funnel the sun's rays to the point where they can incinerate an ant. But his powers of concentration couldn't prevent the soprano from aggravating him throughout the Mass. Not just during the hymns but at every step of the way with her "Amen" or "Father" or "Praise Jesus." Her voice was both timorous and proud.

K knew not what sin the woman might have confessed, but it had to involve self-righteousness arising from vanity. He imagined her mellifluous declarations penetrating the faceless lattice and giving away her identity to the priest. She would have spilled out a bouquet of beautiful sins like a girl splashing on perfume and gracing her homeroom teacher's desk with flowers. There were plenty of beautiful sins: a tear-jerking actress who says "I love you" and then says goodbye; a crooked politician bowing at the waist like an underling to a crime lord, promising the public he will change his ways; crocodile tears—the result of tear ducts stimulated not by pity for the prey but by the act of devouring it; expensive wine drunk on the pretext of toasting the needy. Think of all the flowers of evil in the gardens of this world masquerading as beauty; they're so alluring—can't we snap them off and take them home? Isn't it beautiful sin that leaves angels with their wings cruelly broken? Didn't Snow White die from eating the luscious poisoned apple?

The woman was shrilling now, a cat in heat submitting to a wily tom. The "Amen" she moaned felt like "Hold me"; "Praise be to Jesus" sounded like a vampish "*Love* it"; "Father" felt like "Oh, honey." These siren tones resound in all the places where people are cleansed of their sins—temples, cathedrals, churches—like the outcries of nameless women penetrating the thin walls of rooms in nameless inns. Beautiful sins are pandemic in television, broadcasting, print, music, the fine arts, on the Internet. They rage throughout the globe like a plague, infecting hospitals, schools, universities, families, the National Assembly, the Blue House, toupeed dictators, terrorists. Bedeviled by the fruit of original sin, so delectable and tempting as it imparts knowledge of good and evil, people inject themselves or they strap on explosives for a journey from terror to a dreamed-of Heaven.

K's desultory thoughts were brought under control by the

sermon. He recognized the text as Matthew 24, in which the disciples ask Jesus about the start of the calamities:

"Tell us," they said, "when will this happen, and what will be the signal for your coming and the end of the age?"

Jesus replied: "Take care that no one misleads you. For many will come claiming my name and saying, 'I am the Messiah'; and many will be misled by them. The time is coming when you hear the noise of battle near at hand and the news of battles far away; see that you are not alarmed. Such things are bound to happen; but the end is still to come. For nation will make war upon nation, kingdom upon kingdom; there will be famines and earthquakes in many places...

...and as lawlessness spreads, men's love for one another will grow cold... and then the end will come."

The priest's coughing in the confessional had transformed into passion as he quoted these eschatological prophecies from the Bible.

Such calamities were taking place at this moment, the priest was saying. "Consider this, my brothers and sisters. All over the globe war is breaking out, terrorism is on the rise, and pandemics are raging—even animals are falling victim and being slaughtered on a mass scale. Some 3 million babies are killed each year through abortion, and there are terrible droughts and earthquakes." Last night's earthquake, he continued, the strongest in the country's history, was a signal that the end is near. But we shouldn't be deceived by false prophets; instead we should fuel our lamps and wait for the genuine Christ, like the wise virgins awaiting their bridegrooms.

The priest was fearmongering, thought K. By emphasizing the worst possible circumstances—sickness, fire, and other disasters—the priest came across as a religious insurance salesman trying to peddle a policy. Even if last night's earthquake was the strongest in the nation's history, even if war was a constant threat, and even if drought and epidemics were raging across the globe, the priest's emphatic conclusion that the end was near sounded more like his own phobia than a prediction to be taken seriously. The aspect of this biblical scene that captured K's interest was the passage about the false prophets and false Christs who were misleading the people.

On the wall behind the altar was a bronze cross bearing Jesus and a dove. The dove, representing the Holy Spirit, was descending from the poignant image of the dead Jesus. K found himself returning to the conundrum that had started yesterday with the alarm clock, to his conclusion that his wife was fake, and to his acceptance of H's two experiments, and to his recovery of his identity through the old photos of JS and his mother. But the mysterious phenomena were continuing, as were the delusions involving simulated realities manifested in body doubles produced with all the skill of undetectable counterfeit currency. So, was that image on the wall a symbol of the real Jesus, or a model of the fake Christ that Jesus had prophesied? And if what Jesus had said was true, then wasn't he asserting that when the end was near, a false prophet would appear in the guise of a false Christ?

K's suspicions had been raised another notch. *Is God the father whom I believe is the great creator of all the Universe and of humanity, or is he simply the mortal body of a fake God disguised as God the father? And is the Jesus I believe in the savior of humanity, or is he an anti-Christ, no different from a real doll intricately fashioned out of silicone, or instead of a fake human is he an evil spirit manifest in the flesh, commanding the power to work miracles?*

The devil who had tempted Jesus during his forty-day fast in the wilderness knew the law better than any prophet; he had led Jesus to an overlook and displayed for him all the kingdoms of the world, saying that all that power and glory he had received, and all of it he would give to Jesus. Did that mean that all the kingdoms, all the nations of the world belonged to the devil? And if power came from the devil and not from the barrel of a gun, and if political power controlled us, then weren't we under the control of the devil?

And if Jesus' first proclamation was true, if the Kingdom of Heaven was near, then weren't we citizens of Heaven? And if so, then wasn't the Antichrist making us slaves of earth by promising empty power and glory, by tempting our spirits with the same sweet theorizing and clever lies with which he had tempted Jesus?

The sermon ended. The woman behind K continued with her "Amen" and her "Praise be to Jesus," but K was so immersed in his thoughts that she no longer bothered him. He gazed at the cross, no longer conscious of the ongoing Mass. The cross. Where Jesus had died to atone for our sins. A simple structure—two lengths of wood crisscrossing at a 90-degree angle. A registered trademark of Christianity, a guarantee of authenticity. The dead Jesus, his two hands nailed horizontally, his two feet nailed vertically, the barcode of Christianity.

Suddenly K thought of the Möbius strip. A mathematical shape embedded in a three-dimensional space, so called because it was first proposed by the German mathematician of the same name. A continuous one-sided surface formed by twisting one end of a long, narrow rectangular strip 180 degrees about its longitudinal axis and attaching this end to the other. This strip has several characteristics. If you trace a path starting from the inside of the strip, you will soon end up on its outside; and if you start your path on the outside, you'll soon be back on the inside. The effect of this contradiction is that you can't distinguish inside from outside, or beginning from end—the strip is a perfect continuum.

And the cross is exactly the same—can't tell inside from outside, beginning from end, or right from left—it's a Jesus strip. The two members of the cross intersect, but the image of Jesus has no boundary between inner and outer, beginning and end, alpha and omega. But doesn't the Antichrist also use that cross as his trademark? Just like counterfeiters focus all their efforts on faking the authenticity of the brand?

So there he was again—was the Jesus K believed in the real Christ or the Antichrist, that is, the devil?

K felt more confused than ever. At the same time he realized the highlight of the Mass had arrived. The communion—the receiving of the holy body, originating in the Last Supper. Partaking of the small wheat wafer that symbolized the body of Jesus—this was K's favorite part of Mass, one of the main reasons he attended. Even though he didn't believe that the wheat wafer was the body of Jesus manifest, he drew comfort from the sacrament, and on rare occasions even the ecstasy of being in the presence of the supernatural. But in his present confusion he didn't feel the heart-throbbing anticipation he usually experienced as he fell in line to receive the holy body.

The Escher woodblock print *Möbius Strip II* came to mind.

The red ants on the strip will never arrive at their end point. Because the strip has no starting point.

"The body of Christ," said the server as K arrived in front of him. Glancing at K's face, he deposited a wafer in K's palm.

"Amen," said K before placing the wafer in his mouth as he withdrew from the altar. He returned to his pew, but without the familiar feeling of ecstasy.

"I'm an ant," he murmured as he tasted the host dissolving on his tongue. *I'm an ant on a Möbius strip. With no inside or outside, no beginning or end. It looks like a rectangle but in reality it's a strip that's twisted 180 degrees and connected at the ends.*

To K it was this contradictory virtual reality, this duality, that was twisted 180 degrees.

From behind he heard the woman return to her seat and moan as if she had lost her mind. "Amen, amen, aaaamen. . ."

7:42 p.m.

The pager on the table gave a shudder and buzzed—the spaghetti was ready. K went to the counter, picked up his coffee and seafood spaghetti, and returned to his table. With his wife returning late from her mother's, he should eat before he returned home.

It was near the church, a small restaurant offering tasty meals. The seafood was fresh, and the melted cheese was scrumptious. K had a voracious appetite, but his mind was not on the spaghetti.

What was he to do about his guilty feelings? He had visited an illicit place where a little kiss could lead to who-knows-what, but the main anxiety was his conflicted feelings for JS. To that charge he found himself guilty not of a misdemeanor but a felony—he had broken a basic human taboo. Could that sin be dismissed by a few minutes of confession, three recitations of the Lord's Prayer, and a reading from the Bible? You can pry out a nail but the hole remains. He felt like a smuggler who has delivered his goods and no one but the recipient is the wiser.

Tasting the scraps of his unresolved feelings, K looped the spaghetti around his fork and ate mechanically. He thought about the start of Mass, when the parishioners reflect on the sins they have committed, confessing to God the Father that they have sinned in thought, word, and action, then pounding their chest three times while saying, "It is my fault, my fault, my most grievous fault." It's a public apology, an admission of guilt and a self-sentencing, a declaration that the fault for one's sins lies solely with oneself, and likewise the responsibility.

A shudder ran through K. *That's right—my guilt feelings are not the fault of Sailor Moon and my sister JS, they are my fault alone.*

Mea culpa—a phrase K had heard the priests use when he had gone to church with his mother. Back then the priests didn't look at the congregation but focused on the crucifix on the wall as they recited the liturgy in Latin from beginning to end: *Mea culpa, mea maxima culpa.*

Among the unfamiliar Latin expressions K remembered this one clearly. The priests beating on their chests in contrition and swaying as they chanted this phrase—K had thought they were singing and dancing. He was left with the image of butterflies struggling free of their cocoons. Only later did he learn the meaning of the phrase.

He put down his fork and muttered, "It all starts with *mea culpa.*" Until now he had thought that the conundrum starting yesterday morning was a virtual reality in which he had been deceived, controlled, manipulated, and brainwashed—a reality beginning with his wife and extending to his daughter, the puppy, the cell phone, the matchbox, his sister-in-law, his resurrected father-in-law, the risqué woman, the phone-finding, insurance-peddling designated driver, party B, H's wife, H's nurse, Professor P, his sister JS, the anchor woman and her flasher clone at the coffee shop window, and Sailor Moon.

But, he thought as he looped more spaghetti about his fork, in the center of this conundrum was he himself. The point of departure for all his suspicions about the others—was his wife a spy, his father-in-law a fake, the exhibitionist woman a surveillance operative, the designated driver a tracker, the puppy a counterfeit, and professor P, who was he anyway?—had to be the possibility that he was not actually K. Maybe that was the missing clue, maybe it was K who had been replaced in this virtual reality. Maybe K was the fake, the knockoff, the clone, the tracker, the artificial man. This mysterious reality he was experiencing was his fault, his most grievous fault. As this thought registered, K pounded his chest three times, hard.

I am not myself. I am no longer myself. Someone or something kidnapped me during that cryptic hour and a half on Friday night. Gave me a new face, planted a chip inside my head with all my genetic information—mind and body—cloning me. All my DNA—with 99 percent accuracy. Because a 100 percent perfect match is impossible. And it's that one percent error that made the alarm clock go off at 7 a.m., that ruined my intimacy with my wife, that made the puppy bite me, that resurrected my father-in-law.

His father-in-law must have attended K's wedding fifteen years ago after all. And so K's confusion at his father-in-law's appearance at the wedding yesterday was caused by the one percent error. In other words, he was not the real K. Which would explain his lust for JS. Humans are not animals. Otherwise, how could he have lusted so violently for his own sister? The reason was simple—and unexpectedly so. The K of right now was no longer K. And therefore JS was not the sister of his present, imperfectly cloned self—she was no longer related to him. And the intense lust he had felt toward JS, this familiar other, was not a moral transgression, a breaching of a taboo, but instead a conventional sexual urge involving a man and a woman.

The fault is all through me. Mea culpa, mea maxima culpa.

Finally it was all clear. K was a replacement. In the blink of an eye, a controller, an invisible hand, a Big Brother, a Third Man— whatever you want to call it—had taken his soul with the alacrity of a purse snatcher and his body had been replaced.

K put down his fork, his spaghetti only half finished.

K was no longer K. But then who was he?

He went to the counter, ordered cappuccino, then returned to his table with a pager. He would have to wait for the line of people wanting coffee who had ordered ahead of him.

Suddenly he thought of the letter JS had given him, the letter in response to which she had told him three times that she was sorry (and "*very* sorry" the last of those times). He had no memory of writing that letter. But hadn't he seen that the handwriting was his? And one's handwriting, like a fingerprint or one's blood type, was absolutely reliable for identification.

It must have been the real K who had written that letter. But that information was missing from the chip implanted in his brain, and that's why he didn't remember it.

The pager shuddered to life. K brought the cappuccino back to his table, and retrieved the letter from his pocket. There on the envelope was JS's name and address. His name was missing. He turned the envelope over. There it was—but the return address was utterly different from that of the apartment where K now lived. He scrutinized the postmark—the date was more than three years ago. He pulled out the letter and began reading.

It's been a long time, Sister. How have you been? I keep telling myself I should get in touch, but I never have. I'm sorry, Sis.

Already the real K's writing irked him. Phony greetings and social niceties such as "Sorry, Sis" and "It's been a long time, Sister" were not his style. Did that mean that K1, the real K, had more feeling than K2, the here-and-now K?

He continued down the page:

YD must be getting big—he's in fourth or fifth grade, I guess. I know his uncle should check on him from time to time, but it hasn't worked out the way I wanted.

So far the letter read just like JS had described it. K2 saw these trite, sugar-coated expressions for what they were—a weasel's phony attempt to gain JS's sympathy.

I feel like I'm always so busy. But anyway, here goes—I need a little assistance, Sister. I'm in a bit of a fix. It's a long story. Once the dust has cleared, I can pay a visit and tell you all about it. But if you could scrape up 3 million wŏn, that would be great. I'm not asking for a handout, just give me six months to pay you back. I realize you're not flush your-

self, I just wish I wasn't so desperate... So if you could make the deposit to my account, here's the number... By this Friday would be terrific. Please, Sis, I'm counting on you, you're my one and only sister. Once again, I'm sorry.

And then the closing: *Your one and only brother.*

"What a jerk," K2 muttered. He just couldn't understand. Granted he, K2, was a clone of K1, but judging from this letter, in terms of expression of one's feelings he and K1 differed much more than the one percent error factor. Even though he was a clone of K1, the expression of feelings in this letter was not to his liking—it was a good thing he didn't take after K1 in this respect. But what disgusted K2 even more was the postscript to the letter:

P.S. Sis, these days I often think about Mom, I miss her. Anyway, if anything comes up, you can call me. Here's my cell phone number...

Now he knew the reason for JS's twice-repeated apology—she had turned down K1's request. Looking down-at-the-heels now, three years ago JS must have found it difficult to gather such a large sum of money on the spot. And the matter had been nagging at her ever since—which was why she'd kept the letter all this time.

"Smart thing to do, not sending K1 that money," K2 muttered as he drank his cappuccino. "Even if you had the means. That man's a skunk, JS."

Am I jealous of K1? K2 was a fake, an artificial man, a puppet figure; he had no business criticizing K1, the prototype—where did he get off running down the star of the show? And the lust he, K2, had felt for JS was the result of his envy coupled with hostility toward K1, the precious blood brother of JS and the focus of her apologies. He checked K1's cell phone number, didn't recognize it. But what if he called that number now? Then he could find out if K1 was locked up was locked up or hiding out somewhere.

He had another sip of cappuccino. He had to call K1, but not just yet—he was too frightened.

If K1 were to reveal himself, then what would happen to himself, K2, the fake? If his secret was exposed, if his identity as a fake came to light, who knows, he might be assassinated, like a spy whose cover has been blown; he might turn into dust, like a vampire exposed to sunlight.

Maybe he should take no mind of K1 and just go on living the life of K2, the fake. Yes, there was that small margin of error, but it wouldn't be such a bad thing for K2, the man of the mask, to live life mimicking K1, the genuine article. But K2 was an honest man. Unlike K1, he didn't pretend to be compassionate, was not a sentimentalist. K2 was a levelheaded intellectual, a squeaky-clean banker. And now that he knew about K1's existence, if he continued to exist as K1 and had sex with K1's wife, allowed himself to be called Father by K1's daughter, drank with K1's friend H, and felt lust toward K1's sister JS, then that made him an unforgivable outcast, a devil incarnate.

But if he called K1 and met with him and if they could test the waters of each other's situation, exchange views, and then go back to where they belonged, that would be the righteous thing to do, it would be proof of K2's integrity.

Everything made sense now. Inspiration had struck—all the confusion of the last two days could clear up in a flash. He opened his cell phone and entered the number from K1's letter. He heard one ring, two, three. He liked odd numbers and waited until the fifteenth ring, and when no one answered, he ended the call. He wondered briefly if the number had changed, then realized there'd been no recording to that effect—it must still be a working number. Maybe then K1 was being held incommunicado somewhere?

K2 gulped the rest of his cappuccino, but just as he was about to get up, his phone rang. A number came up on the screen—K1's number, the one he had just tried. He breathed in deeply to steady himself, then took the call. But what would happen if he spoke first? And so he waited. But his counterpart was of like mind, and the silence continued an extra moment.

"Hello."

A chill went up K2's spine—it was his own voice he was hearing. Granted, there was always something unfamiliar about his own voice whenever he recorded himself practicing English conversation. But now that voice was absolutely familiar, the voice of K, and it pierced his consciousness. Still he didn't answer.

"Hello," came the voice a second time. It was more guarded now, almost an undertone. "Who's there? You called me, so say something."

The tone was coarse and threatening, the voiceprint of a criminal, a tone K2 had never used. But the voice itself was identical to K2's. The two men had never met, but their selfsame handwriting and voiceprints made it clear that K1 was K2's prototype.

"Damn it, who the hell are you?"

K2 could no longer remain silent. "Mr. K?"

K2's silence had had an effect. When K1 answered, there was confusion in his voice. "Yeah. And who are you?" he growled, still on guard.

"Well." For want of anything better K2 decided on a white lie. "JS asked me to call."

"JS. JS… who's that?"

"She's… your sister," K2 faltered.

"Yeah, she's my sister," said K1, his tone finally thawing. "What's your connection with her?"

"Why don't we meet and then I can tell you."

"Okay, sure, why not." K2's dry, methodical tone had taken the edge off K1's tone. Was it anticipation K2 now heard? "When's best for you?"

"How about now—if it's all right with you?"

The more they spoke, the more K2 was convinced that K1's voice, albeit coming through an instrument pressed to his ear, was his very own.

"What the hell, why not? Bum like me, it's not like I got places to go, people to see. Come on over. Just so happens I'm having myself a drink. You can join me."

K2 had an inkling about the reason for this 180-degree change of attitude.

K1 offered detailed directions and K2 composed a sketch map in his mind.

"I should be there inside an hour," K2 said matter-of-factly.

"As long as you get here before the night's over," chuckled K1. "I'll be waiting." He ended the call.

K2 needed a cigarette to help him think things through. No turning back now. Had he made a wise decision? Meeting his prototype, K1—wasn't he contravening the invisible hand, breaking one of Big Brother's tacit rules, committing an act of blasphemy?

Even so. Taking a cigarette from his pack, K2 shook his head. The dice had been thrown. If he was being manipulated by an invisible hand according to plan, and assuming he had no say, then maybe this meeting with his prototype was the next item on the schedule.

Just as K was taking his first drag, his chair shook violently. Had someone pushed him? The next moment he was tumbling to the floor. Everywhere he heard rattling. People were screaming and the bottles of wine from the display on the wall were shattering on the floor. A woman was sprawled next to him. K2 watched as a shard of glass penetrated her calf, bringing a tiny sprout of blood.

"It's an earthquake!" someone shouted. Next a light fixture fell from a chandelier. No one was hit—good. And then a fishbowl toppled to the floor in front of him and broke, leaving tropical fish flopping about. The restaurant looked like a shipwreck and felt like a rudderless ship about to sink into the streets bobbing outside. In a split second, earth looked like it had turned into ocean.

A sign snapped free of a building across the street and cartwheeled through the air like an autumn leaf before crashing to the pavement beside a man clinging for dear life to a utility pole. People were shrieking. And then the lights went out—to K2 it felt like a civil-defense blackout. But only the restaurant seemed to be affected, and because the streetlights were still on, K could see about the interior. He heard sobbing and then everything grew unbelievably still, the earth once more settled on its axis.

The cigarette was still burning between his fingertips, the ash was intact. A single draw on a cigarette, that's how long the earthquake had lasted, 30 seconds at most. But the shock was horrific, the force like nothing he had ever felt. K2 could now appreciate the scale of last night's earthquake, the strongest the country had ever experienced.

K picked up his chair, sat back down, and surveyed the chaos of the thirty-second event. He felt he was watching a live broadcast of the earth and its crust had folded back on itself like a Möbius strip, its mountain chains, its axis, its continents all contorted. The lights came back on. Still in shock, covered with dust shaken loose from the ceiling, the patrons clamored and wept and barked out reports on their cell phones.

Why all the commotion? The fear and shock the others were experiencing were nothing compared with the effects of a disturbing nightmare, the despair that comes from knowing you're in the throes of dream trickery and you need to wake up but you remain locked in the dream, total isolation as you try in vain to utter a single scream. Compared with such terror, the aftermath of this earthquake was paltry.

K2 thought of earth as a suicide bomber committing an act of terror against humanity. Who was the invisible hand that controlled this raging terrorist globe? Was it the Christ spoken of by the priest in his sermon—the Christ who appears when the end is near—or was it the Antichrist?

K2 calmly finished his cigarette. He went to the counter and paid, the cashier weeping as she accepted the money and gave K2 his change. Her hand was bleeding.

Outside K came across dark shapes lying in the street, looking like the carcasses of huge beasts. They were trees uprooted by the tremors.

9:12 p.m.

There was an eerie silence to the side street. It was directly opposite Yongsan Station, and K2 had expected the area would still be bustling at this time of night. But the reality was very different. THIS AREA OFF LIMITS TO MINORS—a large sign posted where the side street began.

On the other side of the main street, however, face to face with a phalanx of riot police, displaced residents were demonstrating against a redevelopment project. An occasional Molotov cocktail flew through the air, drawing in response a tear gas canister from the police.

On his way here K2 had come across all manner of damage from the earthquake. No large-scale damage — no elevated express-ways collapsing, no pavement buckling — but the city looked like a war zone. Run-down buildings had been reduced to rubble and res-cue teams were searching for people trapped in the debris. The air was filled with the blare of fire engines responding to fires sparked by downed power lines, the wail of ambulances rushing to tend to those injured by the fallen trees and toppled utility poles, the over-turned cars and dislodged signs. People thronged outside the build-ings that were still standing, looking like a mass of sniffing field mice. Police cruisers were parked at every corner, lights flashing, on guard against the unlikely event of looting.

To K2's eyes, the damage looked no worse than that sustained by a fishing village hit by a tidal wave breaching the jetties. The city was unfazed by the chaos of objects falling, plummeting, breaking, collapsing, turning upside down, distorting, colliding, shaking — it looked like a roller coaster just returned from its dizzying circuit. Its stolid composure exaggerated the peculiar stillness of the side street K2 now entered. He felt like he was entering a ghost town, a war-time buffer zone.

The side street extended some 200 yards straight to a T-intersection and was flanked with identical structures — same height, same size. Each structure was fronted with a large display window like that of a dress boutique, making K2 wonder if he had come across Fashion Row. But a closer look revealed a different real-ity. Festive lights illuminated women who were virtually naked, var-iously sitting, standing, moving, dancing, and singing. Not every-day scenes of eating, drinking, watching TV, or sleeping, but rather the deliberate actions of women exhibiting themselves — a kind of performance art. One woman brazenly beckoned to K as he walked along, another pressed herself up against the glass, legs spread, bot-tom swaying back and forth. The street was like a giant aquarium, the women floating inside their glass cubicles resembling multicol-ored tropical fish in diverse shapes, kept for entertainment purpos-es. It was a brothel district, K2 finally realized. A man could take his pick of the women, just as he might choose among items of cloth-ing, articles of merchandise, or food items on a menu. The street was a meat rack, a human marketplace—a harlot row.

K2 could have himself a leisurely stroll, but other men, eyes glaring like those of rutting animals, hands in pockets to rein in their surging manhood, slunk about seeking women of servitude to suit their tastes. Still others were simply window shopping, indulging in the gratification of a free show by sex slaves. The women could tell the sugar daddies from the cheapskate gawkers. The former they might spur on with a whip-cracking gesture, but to the perverted oglers they offered their backsides, buttocks spread to expose their anus, or pretended to pee into a chamber pot.

K2 ambled down the street, checking out each and every establishment. The women, instinctively realizing he was not a temptable sort, more or less ignored him. And rightly so, because K felt no stimulation from these women—no arousal, no interest. They were delicately adorned and made up, but in the end were paper flowers rather than living specimens. He would have dispensed with his inspection, except that he'd been instructed to look for a certain establishment.

The trouble was, except for a few glitzy neon signs, most of the establishments were anonymous. The earthquake seemed not to have been felt here—no broken windows, no scattered debris, the street quiet as an incubator for preemies, clean as though hosed down by a street sweeper.

Not until he reached the end of the street did he find the sign he was looking for—Wŏlmae. Inside, a few women were at their leisure, playing flower cards, making no attempt to lure or pander.

But at the sound of the glass door opening, they perked up and rose to sink their claws into the customer.

"Well, hello, honey," they cooed. "Where have you *been*, you heartless man."

"I'm sorry to bother you," said K. "I'm looking for someone."

"You just found her, darling," said a women as she stroked K's inner thigh.

"I'm looking for Wŏlmae."

"Wŏlmae? Ch'unhyang's mother, Wŏlmae?" said the woman demurely. "Now I get it. You like your women long in the tooth, is that it, Mister? Why Mommy Wŏlmae? It's mommy's tit you want?"

"If it's tits you want, how about these, you little stud?" another woman chimed in, displaying her bare breasts. "Help yourself, sweetie, they're getting too heavy for me."

"What's your business with Mommy Wŏlmae?" said yet another woman.

"Ranger asked me."

The women's visages froze. Then they exchanged glances with one another, and one of them disappeared toward the back.

"Have a seat," said a woman, offering K2 a chair.

K2 sat.

"Coffee?" said one of the women. Her tone was very different now.

K2 had a sip. And then a rotund woman appeared from where the first woman had disappeared. She was huge. Like the other women, she wore a scoop dress and a glittering necklace. But this woman's necklace was thick as a dog collar.

"Who is it you wanted to see?"

Surprise—the corpulent woman had a soprano voice.

"I'm meeting Ranger here."

The woman gave him a sharp look.

There was something familiar about her. K2 pictured the woman who had emerged from the confessional booth, the woman who had gotten on his nerves with her "Amen" and "Praise be to Jesus" and "Father," the woman who had sung the hymns with her listen-to-me soprano voice. This woman, Wŏlmae, could have been her twin. They were the same person, K2 was sure of it. By now the coincidences had happened so often that K decided to disregard this most recent one. Even if the secret was out—that the devout soprano with her "Amen" was in fact a brothel madam named Wŏlmae—it didn't matter to K2. She probably had more of a conscience than any of the intellectuals who spouted righteousness and yet were united in their corruption, bribery, degradation, hypocrisy, and abuse of power. Hadn't Mary Magdalene, the harlot caught in an act of adultery, been the first to witness the resurrected Jesus, and hadn't she later become a holy woman? Even if Wŏlmae the madam and the amen woman were one and the same, they both deserved admittance to the Kingdom of Heaven.

"Ranger isn't here, and I don't know where he is. What's your business with him, anyway?"

K2 knew she was lying. He decided to cozy up to her.

"I spoke with Ranger an hour ago. He said if I wanted to see him I should come here and ask for you."

Wŏlmae lit a cigarette. She had a ring on every finger, each with a sparkling stone. She thought things over, then said, "Wait here."

On the television was coverage of the earthquake that had just hit. It was a strong one, 6.2, reported the anchorwoman K had seen that afternoon, the woman with the butterfly tattoo. The number of dead was not known but was expected to reach 300. There was a scene of a wailing mother with a dead child in her arms.

Wŏlmae reappeared in a better mood. Had she just gotten off the phone with Ranger?

"All right, you're good," she said to K2. And then, "Hey, Hyangdan!"

A woman with a girlish face who had been watching the television scampered over.

"Take this gentleman to the Chicken Center."

The young woman set off. K2 wanted to thank Wŏlmae but she had already disappeared. He followed the slipper-clad Hyangdan outside.

"Mister," Hyangdan said, fixing K2 with a look. "You look just like Ranger—are you brothers?"

K2 wasn't sure what to say. Hyangdan had a quick eye. Well, it was only natural—he, K2, was Ranger's, that is, K1's, alter ego.

"You're brothers, right, mister?"

"I guess you could say that."

Hyangdan led him around the nearest corner and stopped at a squalid eatery. She turned back to K. "He's in there. So long." And without waiting for an answer she hurried off.

The rotisserie display showed several chickens rotating on a spit. K2 pushed open the door and entered. The interior was dim and all he could see at first was that no customers were in sight. Not that he expected many on a Sunday night after an earthquake—there wouldn't be many stragglers from the trains and the subway.

"Who's there?" The voice was familiar and it came from a partitioned-off area.

K2 craned his neck around the corner and saw a man at a table, his face shaded by a wall sconce. Across from him sat a woman, smoke spiraling from her cigarette. She must run the place.

"I'm here to see Ranger."

"Hey, pal," the man blustered, dropping his guard upon hearing the code name. "About time you got here. Have a seat."

K2 sat down across from the man. The first thing he noticed was the incongruity of Ranger's full beard and Eskimo hood and his T-shirt. The hood and sideburns obscured his face, but K2 instantly sensed he was the very same man as himself. Just like objects have a magnetic field or an electric current, an invisible force by which they exert an equal pull, K2 felt a strong magnetism emanating from Ranger.

His prototype had a plate of fried chicken in front of him, a bottle of *soju* to the side. "How about a drink?" he said, indicating the *soju*.

"I'll have to pass, thanks, I'm driving."

"Then how about a beer? Beer's not going to kill you. Not that I want to force booze down someone who doesn't want to drink."

K2 noticed a tattoo on Ranger's forearm. It looked like a comic book character, but in the dim light he could only make out some details—a red Spandex suit, a helmet, knee-length boots, a belt, and a mask.

"Take a hike, babe," Ranger said to the woman. "We're talking business here."

Without a word the woman rose and disappeared.

Ranger appeared to have had his fill already. The hand holding the shot glass was trembling—was he a late-stage alcoholic? But he still managed to sit straight. He had the canny look of a fighter—a wrestler, perhaps?—who never relaxes his guard.

"So you saw Sister," he said, with no preliminaries.

The woman reappeared with a pint of draft beer for K2, then withdrew.

"That's right."

The men's voices were a perfect match. And if you were to

examine the two men, you would also notice their tone, their body language, gestures, the backs of their hands, fingers, ears, eyes, nose, the jutting Adam's apple—it was undeniable, they were cast from the same mold, fruit of the same womb, identical.

K2 sipped his beer.

"What did she have to say?"

"She said she misses you."

"What the…?" His voice, suddenly ominous, had lowered. He fixed K2 with a venomous look. "And *that's* why you're here?"

Ranger was expecting something and K2 knew it. Three years ago he had sent JS that letter asking her to deposit 3 million *wŏn* in his account. And he'd never gotten a response. So he probably figured she was finally making good on the request and had sent someone around for that purpose. So why would she send a special envoy just to say she missed him?

"That's all she said. She didn't mention anything else."

Ranger dug in his pocket, came out with a jackknife. Pressed a button and a blade snicked out. Then he closed the knife and repeated the action. A poor imitation of a scene from a chintzy old-time gangster movie. K2 was not impressed.

"Oh, there was something else," K2 blurted. "She said she loves you." He couldn't remember for sure if JS had actually said this, but judging from her sucking on his puppy bite, she must have loved her little brother to some extent. So K2 didn't regard it as a lie.

"She misses me. And she loves me, hmm?" Ranger downed another shot of *soju,* then sprung the jackknife blade once more and called out to the woman, "Hey babe, close the door and don't let anyone in."

The woman popped out from somewhere and did as instructed, locking the door for good measure.

"Now listen, pal. I got you in a corner. You can come in here free as the wind, but getting out is a different story. I'm going to ask you one last time. I'll bet JS asked you to deliver the money. You got it from her all right. And once you laid eyes on it you got greedy. But don't you even think about screwing up the delivery. And don't play dumb." And then he prodded K2's chest with the tip of the blade. "I'm going to go through your pockets, and if I find you're holding out, then I'll take it out of you."

K2 smiled. "Look, man, I have no reason to trick you."

Ranger's face contorted—the smile from K2, the utter lack of fear, being referred to as "man." Suddenly the knife shot past K's face and buried itself in the partition behind him. K2 turned and saw the blade lodged in the cleavage of a calendar girl in a bikini. He retrieved the knife and handed it back to Ranger.

"Who are you?" Ranger growled, a ruthless look in his eyes. "Someone's bitch, a P.I.? You came here to take me in, right? The business with JS is bullshit—you never saw her, did you?"

An idea came to K2, a way to pacify Ranger. Why hadn't he thought of it earlier? He reached into his pocket, drew out his wallet, found the two photos JS had given him. He handed the photos to Ranger. Ranger stared at them with a skeptical look. He looked like a sick parrot.

"Hey, babe," he shouted. "Turn on the lights."

K2 heard the sound of a switch and suddenly the interior was brighter.

Ranger silently inspected the photos. As he did so, K2 identified the tattoo on his forearm. It was a Power Ranger. He used to watch the Power Rangers, was fascinated by those superheroes battling to protect the planet from evil forces. They were K2's idols. Among the five of them—Red, Blue, Green, Yellow, and Pink—he fancied himself to be like Red. That Ranger had tattooed himself with one of K2's idols, and that the nickname Ranger itself came from a pleasant childhood memory, gave K2 a feeling of intimacy with the man.

Ranger looked up at him. "Where did you get these photos?"

"From JS."

"So you actually did see her. So you're not someone's bitch, you're not a private dick." But still he glared at K2. "Did Sister ask you to give them to me?"

"No. I borrowed them."

"What for? They belong to us. That's me and my mom when I graduated from grade school. And that one's the three of us at Tŏksu Palace, I think I was in middle school then. Sister found three four-leaf clovers in the lawn there—gave one to Mom and one to me. Said if I took care of it, I'd have good luck. I used to keep it in my wallet. But fuck me if I ever got any good luck out of it."

Ranger seemed to have a more vivid recollection, more detailed memories of the past than K2. For one thing, hadn't he, K2, forgotten about the four-leaf clover mounted on the first page of the album? Then who *was* Ranger? If the two of them were the same person, how could this person remember the clover on the one hand, and completely forget about it on the other?

Jekyll and Hyde. Jekyll, the embodiment of good; Hyde, the embodiment of evil. Dr. Jekyll had concocted a potion that made evil stronger and goodness more pure, and took a sociopathic pleasure in partaking of it, but under its influence he committed murder. The tragedy of it all was that Jekyll ended up turning into the bloodthirsty Mr. Hyde for good, without even taking the potion. Likewise, was Ranger the embodiment of the Hyde within K2, and K2 the embodiment of the Jekyll within Ranger? No—even if Ranger was an outlaw who had slid down a slope of bad luck, K2 could not call him the evil Hyde, and even though he himself had been crime-free, that didn't mean he could call himself the symbol of good. Because Ranger was K2 and K2 was Ranger.

"One thing." Ranger shot K2 a serious look. "What the hell are you doing with a photo of my mom?"

"I borrowed it, that's all."

"That's not what I asked you. *Why* did you borrow it?" Ranger had the peculiar look of a sleepwalker, like he was looking at a ghost. "Your face... why's it so familiar... hey, man... when... we've met before, right?"

"No, never." K2 shook his head. "Today's the first time."

"No way. I recognize you, I'm sure of it. We've met before— and not just once or twice, I swear. Hey babe!"

And there she was in front of them, as if she'd been there all along.

"Take a good look at our pal here. Looks familiar, doesn't he? You recognize him, right?"

She looked long and hard at K2, then answered matter-of-factly. "Are you kidding—he's the spitting image of you. Are you two twins or something?"

Ranger glowered at K2. "Right," he growled. "Looks just like me. Like we're twins. Thing is, I don't have a twin, no fucking way. But apart from the beard, we're peas in a pod. How the hell did you pull this off, did you sell your soul or something?" He downed another shot of *soju*. Instead of having a downer effect, alcohol seemed to sober him up. "What the hell?" he muttered. "Who the fuck are you?"

"Me?" said K2, pointing at himself.

"You see anyone else here besides you? Who exactly are you?"

"I'm K."

Ranger jumped when he heard this. "No shit. That's *my* name." He shot K a look that was both bewildered and dubious. "Different people, same name? Well, so what's your blood type?"

"A."

"How tall are you?"

"Five-nine."

"Where are you from?"

"Seoul."

"Then who's this woman?" said Ranger, indicating the photo from grade school.

"My mother. Your mother too."

"And this woman?" Ranger pointed to JS in front of Tŏksu Palace.

"My sister. Your sister too."

"Then who the hell *are* you?" The voice was louder. Out came the jackknife blade again. "Either cut the crap or you die here and no one finds out."

"I'm you, and you are me."

Ranger brought his face close to K2, so close their noses almost touched, mirror close. The two faces were identical in every respect. And at that moment, what Ranger was thinking was transmitted to K2's mind and K2's spirit was transmitted to Ranger's heart, and both men felt a mysterious rapport.

For K2, looking at Ranger was like looking at himself in the mirror. Like looking at his doppelgänger—a split self, a living apparition, a ghostly double of a living person. Another self, one who is visible to no one but oneself. K2 was face to face with another him. Assuming the two of them shared spirit and soul, then he, K2, Ranger's copy, the soul self, was looking at Ranger, the spirit self, the prototype of K2 in spirit and in soul.

Just then Ranger placed his right palm down on the table, fingers spread, and began stabbing between the fingers with his knife. The tip danced back and forth, managing to avoid the fingers. The little finger—the part from the tip to the first knuckle—was missing. It looked like someone had cut it off. Had Ranger done it himself? Was he trying to show he was a tough guy?

"Show me your right hand," ordered Ranger.

K2 did as instructed, placing his hand on the table.

"Turn it over, like this," said Ranger, pointing to his own right hand.

K2 complied.

"Now spread your fingers. Like me."

K2 did so.

Ranger scrutinized the fingers. "If you're supposed to be me and I'm supposed to be you, then how do you explain *that*?" he said, pointing to K2's intact little finger. "As you can see, I'm missing part of mine."

"But you must have had it originally," said K2, unfazed, "just like me. I'm sure your hand is the same as mine—same fingerprints, same lines on the palm. You cut off part of your pinky and I didn't—that's the only difference. Same holds for the beard—you've got one, I don't, it's only an outward difference."

Ranger grabbed K2's hand and flipped it over. Spreading the fingers, he compared the lines on K2's palm to the lines on his own. It was as K2 had said—the palms were identical, two handprints from the same palm.

"The devil's up to his old tricks," Ranger muttered. "It can't be—it's impossible." Next he stuck out his thumb and compared it with K2's. He scowled in concentration, like an investigator examining a thumbprint. Concluding it was the same as his own, he questioned K2 again. "Damn it, who are you—tell me."

"It's like I told, I'm you. And you're me. It's undeniable."

"Undeniable, my ass. Now listen, you prick." Ranger put K2's hand on the table, this time palm up, spread the fingers, and, as he had done with own hand, began the knife-point dance among the fingers. "This is how I lost the tip of my pinky. So if you're me and I'm you, then your pinky's got to go too—that's fair, eh?"

The blade glittered like the scales of a fish. K2 felt neither threat nor fear, was calm as still water.

Seeing K's imperturbable face, Ranger snapped his fingers. "I just thought of something—if I'm you and you're me, then you know I liked to play rock-paper-scissors when I was a kid, right?"

"Of course."

"And you know I never lost. When I played Sister, the loser had to run up the steps. But not me—I always won. Never lost at slap-match, or at marbles either. Tell you what—let's you and me do rock-paper-scissors," said Ranger. "You win, I forgive you. You lose, you lose your little finger like me."

"But neither of us can beat the other," said K2, shaking his head. "I can't beat you and you can't beat me, no matter how we try."

"What do you mean?" Ranger snarled.

"What I mean is, we're the same, mind as well as body—if you think scissors I think scissors, and if you think paper I think paper."

"You're full of shit. I can beat you. I've never lost—not once. Just wait till I cut off that little finger of yours."

"All right," K2 nodded. He had always started with scissors—in his experience, he won more than half the time that way. And at that very moment, he guessed, Ranger was having the very same thought—same body, same mind.

"Let's go," said Ranger, displaying his right hand and glaring at K2.

K2 went with scissors. Ranger too displayed the two fingers that meant scissors.

K2 considered. After scissors, odds were Ranger would try rock. So K2 should counter with paper. But then he changed his mind—he would stick with scissors.

"There's always a chance," said Ranger grimly. "Here we go—rock, paper, scissors."

K2 flashed scissors. As did Ranger. Ranger groaned as if

waking from a bad dream.

"Let's speed it up. Rock, paper, scissors."

K2 made a fist. Ranger did too.

"Three, four in a row—shit happens. Whatever, I'm good to go. Come on, dickhead. Rock, paper, scissors."

K2, scissors—Ranger too. K2, paper—Ranger as well. No time to think—both men betting on blind instinct. K2 made a fist—Ranger made a fist. No exceptions, no differences. A no-win, no-lose game. After all, there could be no winner and no loser. Just like pi.

Pi—3.14159265358979... Beyond the three it never ends, it's an infinite series of digits. And like this infinite sequence, the two men constituted an infinite mathematical constant, a transcendental number. Not so long ago a supercomputer was put to the pi-computing task for 400 hours. The result—1.24 trillion places. Ranger and K2 were like those never-ending iterations—an irrational number, a two-in-one body.

Finally Ranger accepted that he couldn't defeat K2, nor could he lose to him. He offered his hand to K2 and nodded. "You're right—we can't win and we can't lose, we're a body of one." And then he pointed to the tattoo on his forearm. "Know what this is?"

"It's a Power Ranger. Must be Red—looks red to me, anyway."

"Yep—we were crazy about that show when we were kids."

Ranger had let slip the pronoun *we*. To cover up his blunder he screwed up his face.

"You and I are not two," said K2. "And so we're not 'we.' When the Power Rangers came together, they turned into a single robot that fought the enemy. Remember?"

"Of course." Ranger clapped in delight like a little boy, and laughed. "When those five fighters united, they turned into Mighty Morphin."

"And you and I are like those fighters," said K2. "In normal times we go about our business separate—as Red, Blue, Pink, whoever—but when we have to turn back the bad guys we unite in one body, a robot."

Unite in one body—K2 liked the concept, two or more people coming together in a single body. The reason he and Ranger had been crazy about the Power Rangers was that those individual fighters came together in times of crisis, but did so by uniting into a giant transforming robot.

"So when did we become one?" Ranger asked K2. His gaze was warmer now. "When did we merge? You becoming me, me becoming you—when did we become I?"

"I don't know," K2 said, drinking his beer.

"So when I die, you'll die too."

"Probably."

"*Then* we'll be one?"

"That I don't know."

"Well, you look good. A model citizen—suit and tie. What kind of work do you do, anyway?"

"I work in banking."

"Married?"

"Yeah—have a girl, too."

"Me too—married and a girl."

As they talked they simultaneously had the sensation of turning a key in a door lock and hearing it click open.

"How about that," said Ranger. "We're one body, not separate. Your wife is my wife and my daughter is your daughter—right?"

"I guess so."

"And your wife's name is YH, and your daughter is MS and this year she's around ten or so, I'll bet."

"That's right. I guess there's no getting around it."

"So—K?" said Ranger, calling K2 by his name, the same birth name as his own. "As you can see, I'm a bum. Been in and out of jail. I'm a five-star, five-time-convicted felon. Nothing to be proud of, but you probably figured that out by now. Guess that four-leaf clover didn't do Ranger the crook any favors. But you're me and yet you're miles ahead of me—you're a good citizen, no skeletons in the closet. So if I am bad, you are good—is that possible, K?" Ranger clasped K2's hand and squeezed it, his callused hand as rough as the difficult life to which he had just confessed. "Maybe like Mom said, it's all because people picked the fruit of that tree that God prohibited—what fruit was that, anyway?"

God came naturally off Ranger's lips. Well, nothing surprising about that, thought K2. Ranger, like he himself, must have tagged along with Mother, diligent churchgoer that she was. The Catholic teachings must have survived at the subconscious level.

"The fruit of the tree of good and evil," said K2.

"Okay, now I remember. So if no one had eaten that fruit, then you and I wouldn't know anything about good and evil. And we wouldn't be split apart—we'd be one whole 'I.' Wouldn't that 'I' be the same as the first human created by God? Because that one whole 'I' would be eternal—wasn't born, wouldn't die; no beginning and no end." Ranger's eyes grew moist. Tears formed and began to roll down his cheeks. "You must have loved Mom. I sure did."

But for K2 his feelings for his mother had still not reached the level that he associated with the word *love*. Still, he nodded.

"And I didn't like Dad," Ranger muttered. "All he did was drink and beat Mom. And now here I am a drunken bum, worse than Dad."

The mood was getting too sentimental for K2, and he changed the subject.

"Remember that story Father used to tell us? *Long, long ago there lived a father and son. One day the son pestered his father to tell him a story. And so the father told him a story. 'Long, long ago there lived a father and son...'*"

"Sure do," said Ranger. "And life keeps going round and round, just like that stupid story. The son is born of the father, that father is born of the grandfather, that grandfather is born of his father... And if you climb that ladder all the way to the end, then who is the first father, the father of me? And how was that first father born?"

K2 checked his watch. Almost 10:30. It was getting late. Time to say goodbye.

Ranger had noticed. "So what's your plan?"

"I have to go home. My wife and daughter are waiting. Same with you, right?"

"I left home a month ago," Ranger said as he gnawed on a

piece of cold chicken. "One day I just felt my wife was a fake. My daughter too. Like someone had replaced them. So I'm just hanging out, like you see here. Got all the girls I want, they can all play the little woman. Wŏlmae too—you met her, right. She thinks I'm the man. But I'm the man for *all* of them."

"I have to go," said K2, getting up.

Ranger motioned him back down. "Before you go—give me one of those photos. Then we each have one to remember the other guy by."

"Which one do you want?"

"This one," said Ranger, indicating the graduation photo taken in front of the school. That woman, the woman they had called Mom, wherever she was now, was hugging K2/Ranger from behind.

"All right. And I'll take this one," said K2 as he put the Tŏksu Palace photo in his wallet.

"Next time?"

"Sure—why not."

"And if we don't recognize each other, all we have to do is show the photos."

The photos—tokens, markers of one's identity, relics from history books. A pair of objects that fit together, by means of which a pair of secret envoys could recognize each other. When next they met, K2 and Ranger would produce those photos and know they were not two but one.

"Take care," said K2 as he rose.

"Glad I met you," said Ranger, wrapping an arm around K2's shoulder as he got up. "I've got the tab. But maybe it's better if we don't meet again—what do you think?"

The two men were exactly the same height, as if cut from a blueprint.

"If you get hit by a car, I will too. If I stab someone with this knife, you'll hurt somebody too. I die, you die too. It's better if we pretend we don't know each other. No need to explain—otherwise people would take us for a couple of loonies."

Ranger walked K2 to the door.

Rain was spattering onto the pavement. Farther off, lights

were going out, but here in the brothel district, they only brightened as the night darkened, like creatures glowing in the dark.

"Hang on—it's not the time of year you want to get caught in the rain." So saying, he hurried off.

K2 gazed blankly at the rainy scene. A family of rats darted out from a small flowerbed and disappeared down the alley. He'd never seen so many rats before. He imagined the Pied Piper luring rats to a riverside outcrop, where they tumbled into the river to drown.

Ranger reappeared with an umbrella. "Here, use this. Don't want you—I mean, me—catching cold," he chuckled, giving K2 a pat on the shoulder.

Ranger offered his hand.

Why bother? thought K2. But not wanting to turn down the gesture of goodwill, K2 took the hand.

"So long," said Ranger as they shook.

With no further words K2 set off down the alley. He knew Ranger was watching him, but then thought of the story of Sodom and Gomorrah, and not wanting to turn into a pillar of salt, he didn't look back. If the Ranger he had just met at the Chicken Center was another "I," then K2 would soon die. He felt autoscopic, believed the appearance of a doppelgänger presaged imminent death.

Seeing K2, the stripped-down women in the show windows bordering the street whistled, danced, called out to him, lifted their skirts and showed their thongs. One even stood on her head. But K2 walked on, confident even in the face of death. No sight, no sound registered. *There is only me, and I am my own man.*

10:53 p.m.

"Five hundred yards to your destination," K's GPS announced. He had just passed an unlit intersection and turned onto an arterial. He was almost there.

Shops were closing for the night. Vestiges of the earthquake were in evidence along the dark street. Water was bubbling up in places—a water main must have burst.

Rain was still spattering on the windshield. Back and forth went the wipers. The arterial was unfamiliar, and relying on the GPS, K felt like he'd lost his sense of direction. Except for the rare occasions when he went to the remote countryside, he didn't use the GPS. When he had to meet someone it was usually at a place he knew.

And he didn't like this navigational aid to begin with. It made him feel like an idiot with no sense of direction, no capacity for judgment, a puppet dancing on strings. But now it was unavoidable — on his way home he had suddenly changed his mind. For his dialogue with Ranger had awakened him: if he and Ranger were a unified "I," then the same held true of his wife and Ranger's, and his daughter and Ranger's. And his wife and daughter must be clones of Ranger's. Which accounted for K's suspicion that his wife was a fake. And hadn't Ranger complained of the very same feeling?

"I left home a month ago. One day I just felt my wife was a fake. My daughter too. Like someone had replaced them. So I'm just hanging out, like you see here."

Ranger had had the same experience — suddenly one day his wife and daughter feel like fakes. So he leaves home and bums around. But did that mean K's wife was Ranger's wife? And K's daughter Ranger's daughter? And that bite on K's ankle — that was from Ranger's puppy. At the moment of that realization, he stopped, checked the return address in Ranger's letter, and changed direction. There was always a chance it was an old address, but it was the only one he had and he had entered it in his GPS. Instantly the map and directions had lit up on the screen — the direction was opposite the direction of K's apartment.

And now here he was. "One hundred yards ahead turn left," announced the GPS. And appearing at the bottom of the screen, *Two hundred yards to your destination.*

K drove a short distance down the dark, shop-lined street, and a small three-way intersection appeared. He turned left into a residential area where single-family homes had been replaced by apartment buildings.

"Your destination is straight ahead."

The street had narrowed to a point where two cars could scarcely pass. The only light in the immediate vicinity came from a convenience store.

"One hundred yards to your destination."

K's heart was palpitating. He felt like a marathoner approaching the finish line. A range of emotions—anticipation, curiosity, a slight anxiety about meeting his pre-replacement wife. His mouth was dry; he drank some water.

"You have arrived at your destination. Goodbye."

The screen was blank—no more instructions, no more red line leading to the destination. K inspected the place. It was a dry-cleaner's, and it should have been closed at this hour but the lights were still on.

He parked next to a tree with half its branches snapped off by the earthquake, and looked inside the shop. With the surroundings in gloom and the shop brightly lit, K could peep inside yet remain hidden from view. A woman was pressing garments. She must have been short-handed, keeping the business afloat all by herself. She did the pressing with a practiced hand, steam issuing from the press at regular intervals. Pressed clothing hung in a neat row overhead, like slabs of meat at a butcher shop.

To the rear of the shop, in what looked like the living quarters, was a commercial-size washer-dryer. Like its owner, it was still in operation—K could see the tub spinning. On a shelf in front of the woman was a television, to which her eyes returned at every opportunity.

Thin streaks of rain ran down the shop window. The half-open door offered a better view of the interior. The woman wore a T-shirt, appropriate for working a steam press and baggy enough that K could see her breasts. Those breasts looked familiar. And not just the breasts but also her movements and the line of her neck and shoulders as she watched the television, and her face as well. No, she didn't just resemble his wife, she *was* his wife.

It was K's wife working the steam press. Different place, different clothing, different hairstyle, different occupation and surroundings—in spite of it all, this woman running the dry cleaning shop was K's wife, there was no doubt in his mind.

What next? Should he nonchalantly go up to her, like a husband just returned from an outing? Ranger said he had taken off a month ago. How would she react? Would she treat him like an intruder, maybe threaten him with the steam press? Would she scream and call the police?

Or should he return to his apartment, to sleep with his lawfully wedded wife? But wouldn't that be adulterous? Who, then, was K's real wife, the one in the apartment or the dry cleaning woman? And who was K, the man who worked for a bank or Ranger with his stable of women?

Just then a girl appeared. She was holding a little ball. His daughter. From the narrow space behind her mother she came outside, stuck out her hand to see if it was still raining, and looked up at the heavens. Satisfied that the rain had stopped, she threw the ball down the alley. The next moment K saw something scamper after it. It was the puppy, the puppy that had bit him in the ankle. In no time it had returned to K's daughter, ball clenched between its jaws. Yes, it was his daughter, MS, all right. But unlike his daughter at the apartment, she wore her hair in two plaits with a bow. And she looked more perky and cheerful.

Again his daughter threw the ball. It hit the hood of K's car and bounced once on the ground. In no time the dog had scurried after the ball. It had come to rest where a tree branch had broken, right outside where K sat in his car. Instead of retrieving the ball and returning it to its master, the puppy caught sight of K and began barking. It was the bark of a dog that sees its master. Its tail began to wag and it jumped against the side of the car.

K slid down the window and whistled, as he usually did to calm the puppy. But instead the puppy grew more excited, dashed to his daughter, and took the hem of her skirt in its mouth. K's daughter got the message and inched her way to the car. At the broken branch she stopped; she had recognized K.

"Daddy!"

She ran back inside to her mother at the steam press, and the silence of the surroundings was broken.

"Mommy, it's Daddy! Daddy's back!"

The woman glanced at K in the car, then resumed her work as if nothing had happened. His daughter returned to K, the puppy nestled in her arms.

"Daddy!"

Her hand came in the open window and tugged at K's hand.

"Daddy, come on! Let's go in!"

K got out of the car with Professor P's gift from the store and locked the car. The girl held fast to K's hand, as if pinching the wing of a butterfly about to take flight. No way would she let Daddy fly off again.

"How are you doing?" he said to his and Ranger's daughter.

"I missed you, Daddy. Daddy, what's this?"

"It's a present, for you."

"Daddy, you're the best!" she squealed in delight.

K was led inside the shop.

"Look what the cat dragged in," barked the woman. "Where did you slink off to, you bum?" She snorted. "Get a load of this—shaved his beard, prettied himself up in a suit. Must have robbed a bank or mugged someone."

"Mommy," called MS in a mollifying tone, tickling her in the armpit. "Look—Daddy bought me a present." And then to ease the awkward moment, using the narrow passageway behind her mother as a fashion runway she modeled the parka, which was too big but otherwise became her.

"You're going to be the death of me yet—are you going to stand there all night?" she snapped. Her daughter's cuteness seemed to be having an effect. "Get your ass inside, you jerk. And don't let me see you here unless you want that mug of yours pressed. *Aigo*, last person I want to see—bastard!"

A beep came from inside the room to the back—the dryer cycle had ended. The woman set off toward the washer-dryer and found K blocking her way.

"Get your butt back there—scram!" she shouted.

K faltered his way to the rear. Among the garments suspended from the ceiling he could see two rooms set into the back of the shop. One projected out in front of the other—his daughter's room. The other would be for the couple. His daughter was already in front of the mirror in her room, checking herself out in the pair of pants K had brought. The window was at ground level and framed a bed of chrysanthemums—did the owner of the building live back there?

Exhausted, K decided he might as well stay there. He took off his clothes and hung them. Tucked between the two rooms was a bathroom complete with shower. It had long been K's habit to shower before bed. Without hesitation he stripped down and headed for the shower. The shower head stuck out of the wall and there was a plastic curtain to keep water from splashing onto the toilet. He drew the curtain and flipped the switch that operated the on-demand hot-water system. In no time the water was hot.

He began to wash. He felt peace in spite of his exhaustion—it really did feel like he'd returned home after being gone for a month. He soaped himself all over, and as he lathered up with the washcloth he had an erection. It wasn't because of stimulation from the lathering; rather it was the explosive desire he had felt for JS that afternoon, the bubbling magma trying to penetrate the weak point of his crust. He felt like a loaded gun; only the safety was holding him back. All he had to do was pull the trigger.

As he always did in the shower he whistled. But the space was too confined, and instead of resonating, the whistling came out sounding flat.

Finishing the shower, he toweled off in front of the mirror, then looked into the mirror and examined his face. There he was, "I," whether that meant K or Ranger he couldn't tell—but who cared?

Ruffling his damp hair with the towel, he went back out and sat on the spread-out bedding to check the warmth of the heated floor. It was hot from the stone layering of the heat flues. He pulled aside the fabric covering of the tiny clothes cabinet and there were his familiar pajamas. He put them on, lifted the quilt, sat on the sleeping pad on the heated floor.

The scene was partly familiar, partly unfamiliar. On the shelf of the low dressing table rested a small framed photo from their wedding day. The groom was clearly K, the bride obviously his wife.

He found the remote and turned on the television. The anchorwoman was still reporting that the 6.2 earthquake was the strongest in the nation's history. Scenes of the damage appeared intermittently.

The rain had started up again. Through the half-open window K heard raindrops pattering onto the chrysanthemums. And then a siren wailed. Through the hollow door K could hear the woman moving around—she must have finished her pressing and closed up for the night. In his tired state, snug and cozy after the hot shower, he soon dozed off, head cradled in the crook of his arm. How long had he dropped off? Something was pressing him down. His eyes opened. There she was, Ranger's wife and his, squatting over him. He had been beneath the quilt and now he was on top of it. His pajama bottoms were off and he was naked from the waist down. The light in the room was off, but enough light came in from the bathroom. As his head cleared he realized that in spite of himself he was hard and his wife was teeter-tottering above him. So, while he was dozing, she had come back here, rearranged the bedding and positioned K on it, brought the sleeping K's manhood to attention, and had gotten them off and running. It felt kind of like being violated, but he didn't find it unpleasant.

If what Ranger had said was correct, his wife hadn't seen K for a month. And so she was making up for lost lust, and even though she was forcing him into the act, he understood. You could compare conjugal relations to licking a stamp—all you do at first is lick it, but as time goes by, the gum fails to hold and you have to apply the glue stick. Meaning the couple has to make an extra effort to bond. In the end K and his wife were bartering their bodies, each to the other, renewing their conjugal contract like two debtors paying an installment on a loan.

The last two nights K had experienced a ghastly, chilling sensation from his wife's body, leaving him feeling like a pervert making love to a body in a morgue. And then there was the silicone feel of Sailor Moon's flesh. But now his wife's body was warm, intimate, familiar.

K reached inside his wife's nightshirt, felt her breasts. He had never done this before, but it felt so satisfying. Her breasts were plump and firm, the nipples thick and sensuous. He sucked on those nipples like a baby.

A moan escaped her. "Where have you been, you prick?" came her feverish voice.

"Here and there."

"Here and there where, you bastard, you left me high and dry. You didn't get yourself in trouble, did you?"

"No."

The rain was heavier, its swoosh audible through the half-open window. K looked toward the window, feeling someone was watching. But instead it was a stray cat that was taking in the scene.

"No-good slimy bum, wish I could beat the shit out of you. You screwed up, didn't you—you screwed up, you fucked up, you prick. Say it. You screwed up, you fucked up."

His wife's body was heating up. *You screwed up, didn't you?* It wasn't a question waiting for an answer but an orgasmic outcry. The magma bubbling inside him since that afternoon had found the weak spot in his crust and was shooting out.

"You screwed up, didn't you. Fucked up. Ahhh, fucked up."

"Yes... I... fucked... up." And finally the bursting tension was released. She too shot up like a kite into the heavens. And with their barter completed, K and Ranger's wife and his apartment wife rebonded as a couple, recommitted themselves, took each other in their arms. Like Professor P and his lost half, Olenka, newfound K and his newfound wife had come together as an eternal one. Woman had become the rib of man and turned back into the clay of humanity.

MONDAY

7 a.m.

(PLAY)

What the hell? K groped the fuzzy boundary between sleep and wakefulness for an answer—what had awakened him?

His alarm clock. The strident ring a desperate cry letting the world know of its existence. Again the shrill clamor.

Dammit! K didn't like being woken up. He fumbled at the nightstand, found the alarm clock, silenced it.

He wasn't fully awake. But he was conscious enough to splice the snapped filmstrip of his interrupted sleep, and he closed his eyes.

Hey! The alarm was telling him it was time to get up. He forced his eyes open, checked the display on the clock. 7 a.m. sharp. 7 a.m. He groaned. Time to rise. Time to get his butt in gear—get up, get ready, get off to work. He sat up. (STOP)...(FF)...(PLAY)

K opened his eyes and looked about. He was in his familiar apartment. He examined his surroundings. The polka-dot curtain, the Renoir reproduction on the wall, the hollow in his wife's pillow, the strands of her hair, the rumpled bedding, the nightstand, beneath the lamp the framed photo of their wedding, the door to their bathroom, the wardrobe with the door half open and revealing his wife's dresses.

The familiar bedroom was his. But K was confused. What about last night at the dry cleaner's? What about his lovemaking with Ranger's and his wife? He had definitely fallen into a sleep deeper than that of the dead, embracing his wife number two— how had he been transported through space back here? Had someone spirited him away in the middle of the night and laid him down here? Or was it all just a dream? Was it a part of the simulation, the fake reality, that was supposed to have been erased? Was he wandering?

Ringwanderung—in whiteouts and times of limited visibility you may have the illusion that you're heading straight for your destination, when actually you're going around in circles. Was that what he was doing last night? Like ants on a Möbius strip, was he on an infinite journey, from inner to outer and back to inner, a journey without beginning or end—and last night was an inconceivably short instant in that journey?

But today was Monday and he no longer had the luxury of time to lapse into confusion. If he didn't get his ass in gear, he'd be late for work.

He sat up. He was wearing his pajama top, but—like last night at the dry cleaner's—no bottom, and his briefs were missing too; he was buck naked from the waist down. So then, the woman K had had sex with last night—was she the dry-cleaner wife or the wife in the kitchen preparing his breakfast—making toast, chopping vegetables, brewing coffee? He got out of bed and headed for the bathroom.

(STOP)...(FF)...(PLAY)

He felt the urge and sprang out of bed, heading for the bathroom. Tapping his full bladder, he watched the yellow stream foam up in the toilet bowl, noticed the alcohol odor. He flushed the toilet...

(STOP)...(FF)...(PLAY)

At first glance a trivial detail but ultimately a giveaway of the elaborate production that Big Brother was staging.

(STOP)...(REW)...(PLAY)

But before he could unwind, there remained the bathroom ritual. V, his signature aftershave—somebody had switched it. One petty detail, but it gave away the elaborate production that Big Brother was staging. But the aftershave would have to wait. First things first. He squeezed a large dollop of toothpaste onto his toothbrush and started brushing.

(STOP)...(FF)...(PLAY)

Oops—he had drawn blood. He stuck a piece of tissue to his chin. There—a nice clean shave. He looked much more cheerful now. With warm water he removed the remnants of lather. Then he picked up the troublesome aftershave.

(STOP)...(FF)...(PLAY)

The aftershave was strong stuff. It felt like a branding iron on the nicks and scrapes. Then came an electric buzz that left his face momentarily numb. And the fragrance, so powerful he didn't need cologne.

But, he shook his head. It wasn't his V.

The smell...

(STOP)...(FF)...(PLAY)

The smell was like a combination of Olenka's perfume, JS's body odor, Sailor Moon's fragrance, and the perspiration odor from his dry-cleaner wife.

He checked the label. Brand D. Now he was really confused. V was the brand he'd always used. The day before yesterday it had been changed to Y, and then yesterday to X, and now this morning, a brand he had never heard of, D.

What was happening? And then it occurred to him.

The Third Man, the invisible hand controlling all of these games, hadn't been supplied with correct information about K's aftershave. Big Brother...

(STOP)...(FF)...(PLAY)

K stepped into the shower, turned on the water. Last night, if memory served him correct, he had used a shower with an on-demand hot-water system, but...

(STOP)...(FF)...(PLAY)

With the aid of the magnifying mirror he carefully pinched the hairs with his fingers. Each pluck left a tiny sting, as from an injection.

(STOP)...(FF)...(PLAY)

His wife was at the sink chopping spinach. For breakfast K typically had salad.

(STOP)...(REW)...(PLAY)

Light of heart, he returned to the bedroom and got dressed. In the full-length mirror stood an ordinary businessman. Trousers properly creased. From among his many ties he chose his favorite red one. This preference dated back to his childhood, when he liked to don the red uniform of Red, his idol among the Power Rangers he was so crazy about.

Whistling, he went out to the living room. Dazzling autumn

sunlight flooded through the picture window that looked down on the main street.

His wife was at the sink chopping spinach. For breakfast K typically had salad—lettuce, celery, tomatoes, spinach, broccoli, onions—with a banana thrown in for good measure.

K entered the kitchen. "Good morning, honey."

His wife turned and answered. "Oh hi—did you sleep well, dear?" It was his wife, without a doubt.

"Sure did."

K poured a mug of coffee and sat down at the table. He took a sip and savored it. *Good old coffee.*

Between sips he picked up the newspaper.

Record 6.2 Earthquake Hits, 8:32 p.m.

(STOP)...(FF)...(PLAY)

His wife turned to him. "Where were you last night when we had the earthquake?"

"At a restaurant near the church, after Mass. I was having spaghetti."

"I was so frightened. The whole building was shaking, and there was a fire in one of the apartments across the way. Be careful today—they say there might be some strong aftershocks. Apparently there's an exodus of people driving down to Taejŏn and farther south. Everybody's buying up emergency supplies. Do you think we should go to a safe zone?"

"What are you talking about? I have to go to work."

"Honey," his wife cooed. "How was it for you last night?"

K played dumb. "How was it for *you?*"

She smiled. "You didn't strike out. What in Heaven's name got into you, anyway? You turned into a Casanova. Hit a home run, knocked me out of the park... Amazing—you're just full of surprises, Mr. Casanova."

K prudently spread open the newspaper, then felt a tap on his shoulder.

"How's the coffee, dear?"

"Good—very tasty."

"Just the coffee?" His wife gave him a wink.

"Coffee's tasty, but you were absolutely delectable, my dear," said K with a poker face.

Just like yesterday morning, here he was playing to perfection his lead role in this large-scale production, this mystery show. A star was born!

(STOP)

8:14 a.m.

Attaché case in hand, K took the escalator down to the subway stop. The lower level also gave access to a department store, a shopping arcade, and a walkway to the terminal from which express buses came and went throughout the country.

K worked in Yŏŭido. From here it was eight stops on the subway to his company. Thirty minutes would get him there with time to spare.

It was Monday morning. Most of the commuters walked briskly through the ant-farm maze, with walkways extending in every direction. They were the worker ants, the breadwinners.

As always, K checked himself out in any available display window to make sure his clothes were tidy and not a strand of hair was out of place. His feet leading him along, he felt like an ant on a Möbius strip.

At the far end of the shopping arcade K encountered a man, Bible in one hand and a sign in the other reading *Believers in Heaven, Doubters in Hell.* The man shouted his message like a prophet in the wilderness, but no one was stopping to listen.

K had a look at the man's face as he passed him by. The man looked familiar. He resembled K's father-in-law and JS's husband. With every squawked phrase he pressed his tongue over his dentures, as if to keep them in place. "Repent, for Heaven is near!"

Past the man, K headed toward line 9. This subway station, the Express Bus Terminal, was the transfer point for lines 3, 7, and 9. The confluence of the walkways to the three subways was a turbulent human tide where currents warm and cold came together.

Line 9 being the newest of the three, it was the deepest underground, five levels down. But K didn't feel like he was going underground; he felt like he was taking a deep-sea submarine. He started down the steps toward the turnstiles. The stairway was flanked by escalators but K preferred the steps.

To his left a woman was coming up the escalator. She wore a familiar dress and familiar sunglasses — the exhibitionist, the woman with the butterfly tattoo, the television anchorwoman. She took her hand from her pocket and swept her hair back, using the gesture to glance at K, and for a brief instant their eyes met. K felt she was responding to his gaze. Where they passed each other, K caught a whiff of the woman's stink. At the same time the woman surreptitiously flashed him a V with her fingers. Whether it was the V for *victory* or simply a bye-bye gesture K couldn't tell. Just as she disappeared at the top of the escalator, K caught sight of a familiar man, also going up. It was the man with the red cap, party B the insurance man, the designated driver. As they passed each other the man doffed his cap and nodded in K's direction.

Now K knew. The gesture was intentional, a silent goodbye. It was an implicit farewell, undetectable by the invisible hand that was keeping K under constant surveillance. And that's when he realized that the V from the butterfly woman also meant goodbye.

The familiar faces kept coming. The next one was the man at Janus, the gay bar. Today he wore a dandy suit instead of women's clothes, but everything about him remained feminine. He was most definitely a well-built man but every gesture, every hand movement was a snapshot of femininity. In his hand was a birdcage, and in the birdcage was a parrot. As the two men crossed paths the parrot began screeching "Janus, Janus."

K felt the parrot was trying to tell him something in bird language. If K were Saint Francis perhaps he could have preached to the bird, but K had been baptized Peter and was unable to converse with avian species.

At the turnstile K took out his wallet with the T-card and tapped the sensor pad. *Beep!* Through he went.

The tracks were yet another level down. He descended the steps. Now there was only an up escalator, and up it came a group of three—K's familiar sister-in-law, the familiar groom, and K's familiar mother-in-law. The bride was in her wedding dress, and the mother-in-law was dabbing at her teary eyes with her handkerchief. The groom grinned in every direction, radiating his Master of Weddings aura. Suddenly a young man in front of K took something from his pocket and tossed it at the groom. Confetti. The groom waved a white-gloved hand in acknowledgment, then drifted up past K and disappeared.

Why were all these characters from the two-day shadow box popping out now, in succession, in the morning rush hour? It was like the end of a play or movie, when all the main characters come together en masse in one climactic scene.

Who would be next? K felt a vague sense of anticipation. Here she came, the "Amen" woman who had transformed into Wŏlmae on Harlot Row. Summer was long gone but she held an exotic fan. As she and K came shoulder to shoulder she gave him a haughty flourish with the fan and whispered "Amen." The sound was like a breath of air sent by the fan, too soft for Big Brother to hear. Yet another privy farewell. K marveled at Wŏlmae's attention to detail—muffling the "Amen" with her ingenious prop.

Next to bob up the escalator was a woman with a parasol. K recognized her at a glance—Professor P, or rather Olenka. Dressed like a woman in a Renoir painting, white opera gloves and all, she gave K an undisguised smile when their eyes met, her hot lipstick standing out.

He wanted to say something—he couldn't simply pass by—and he paused for a moment. But Olenka, pretending to dab at perspiration, placed a finger against her lips—*hush*—before floating away like a ghost ship.

According to Einstein's theory of relativity, if you could speed through the universe faster than light, you could see into the past. And here was K, on a spaceship faster than light, going back through time and space to yesterday, the day before yesterday, a year ago, ten years ago, a hundred years ago, back to the years of our Lord, when

Jesus was crucified at Calvary, back to the years before Christ, to the time of the Garden of Eden—was it to show all of this history that the characters of the last two days had reappeared before him in a dress rehearsal?

K's steps grew heavier. Another group was coming up the escalator. Not real people but a hologram. Were they a family? First came a girl in the winged costume of an angel. She was dancing and playing an angel's trumpet. And then a man in military dress, who looked like the father, saluting. And next to him a beautiful woman with a baby in her arms. Clutched in the baby's fernlike fingers was the string to a red balloon. They looked so happy, like carnival performers dancing in paradise.

It was him and his family, K realized. The girl with the wings and the halo about her head was his sister, JS, now 250 pounds; the man in the army uniform, the father he hated. The woman holding the baby was his departed mother, and the baby with the balloon, K himself. As the woman passed him, K reached out to take her hand and in spite of himself said "Mommy," whereupon the hologram broke apart and K was left holding not his mother's hand but the string to the baby's red balloon. But the balloon too, like a living thing, slid free from K's hand and flew off into the air. Reaching the ceiling, it came to a stop.

K continued down to the platform for the west-bound trains. The overhead display told him the next train would arrive in three minutes. He had a premonition that those three minutes would mark the end of the simulation. This grand production, mobilizing all the performers of the last two days, along with the images from his childhood, would come to an end, and the troupe would appear for a curtain call and make one last bow. And then the curtain would close on this Möbius-like pseudo reality.

Across the tracks stood a girl in a school uniform holding a satchel. The uniform top looked familiar. It had the distinctive collar of a sailor. It had to be Sailor Moon, transformed into a student.

Just then the platform began shaking. K was sent sprawling. There was an ear-shattering roar and one of the walls began to crinkle like a parched leaf. Parts of the ceiling came down, along with their supports. The red balloon sailed free.

"It's an earthquake!" shouted a man sprawled in front of K. The earth was rocking on its axis, sifting out impurities. Smoke came up from the rail bed, like clouds of sulfur billowing from hell.

Flat on the platform, K looked about. The girl across the tracks took something from her satchel. It was the magic wand Sailor Moon had shown him. The girl waved the wand, recited a spell, and turned once in a circle, and suddenly she was Sailor Moon. She had the same yellow hair, the same white gloves, the same red ribbon on her chest, the same knee-high boots as yesterday. Brandishing her magic wand, tiptoeing as if on a balance beam, she began to sing:

> *The moonlight gently enfolding me*
> *Your eyes beholding me,*
> *It is not by chance*
> *That I meet you, my dear,*
> *Among the countless stars*
> *For I am your Magical Sailor Moon.*

It was a spine-tingling performance. And then she dropped something. The magic wand. K spotted it—it had fallen onto the tracks. Down jumped Sailor Moon after it. K checked the overhead display. Thirty seconds until the train arrived. K hesitated, wondering how the train could still operate in the midst of an earthquake.

Sailor Moon grabbed the wand, struggled to free it—it was caught beneath the joint bar.

From the maw of the tunnel came a rumble as the train approached.

K hopped down onto the tracks. He took Sailor Moon's hand. "Get up, quick!"

"No, Leon, we can't. We need the wand, to take care of the Tree of Life."

"Come on!"

From out of the dark tunnel came a beam, like a watchtower searchlight. They had to move fast.

"You can't stay here. For God's sake come on!"

"Sir Knight of the White Rose," said Sailor Moon, the Moon

Nymph. "Leave me and save yourself—hurry!"

But K couldn't leave her just to save his own skin. The simulation was ending and the screen would turn black. K clutched Sailor Moon's hand with a hand drained of energy. Suddenly he felt a surge of power. He looked at his hand, and in that split second it was joined with another hand. The hand of K1, Ranger's hand. Ranger grinned at K2. Finally the two of them had joined in a single "I," K1 and K2 in one complete K. And now, thought that one complete K, it was time to return to alpha, before the universe had split into heaven and earth, it was time to return to the very beginning, to the time before K's father and his father's father, before his father and his father's grandfather, before that grandfather and that grandfather's grandfather, before all those fathers. To the time before the creation of heaven and earth, when the earth was formless and void, before there was any living thing, when the oceans were draped in darkest night beneath primal chaos and omega heaven, when only the Word existed.

(POWER OFF)

Library of Korean Literature
Dalkey Archive Press